Reading Jean Toomer's *Cane*

Reading Jean Toomer's *Cane*

Gerry Carlin

HEB ☼ Humanities-Ebooks

The Author has asserted his right to be identified as the author of this Work in accordance with the Copyright, Designs and Patents Act 1988.

First published by *Humanities-Ebooks, LLP,*
Tirril Hall, Tirril, Penrith CA10 2JE

Cover image © Nicola Allen

The Pdf Ebook is available to private purchasers from http://www.humanities-ebooks.co.uk and to libraries from Ebrary, EBSCO and MyiLibrary.com.

ISBN 978-1-84760-332-6 Pdf Ebook
ISBN 978-1-84760-334-0 Paperback
ISBN 978-1-84760-335-7 Kindle Ebook
ISBN 978-1-84760-336-4 ePub Ebook

Contents

Acknowledgements

Special thanks to Paul McDonald for his editorial skills, and to Nicola Allen for her really helpful comments on a draft of this study, and for the cover art.

1 Introduction

Jean Toomer's *Cane* was published on the 1st September 1923, and would come to be regarded by many as one of the earliest and most original works associated with the cultural movement in African-American literature, art and music called the Harlem Renaissance. In reference works, libraries and bibliographies *Cane* is called a novel, but it is more accurately described as a collection of short stories, poems and dramatic pieces of 'indefinable genre'[1] whose stylistic indeterminacy is part of its unique appeal. Structurally, *Cane* is sub-divided into three sections, set respectively in the agrarian American south, the modern industrialised north, and a final return south. It examines the life of rural folk, modern city dwellers, and their experience of change, diaspora and uprootedness, dealing with taboo topics such as racial mixing, miscegenation and racist violence. Most of the key writers and intellectual figures of the day praised the work, despite being somewhat awed by its exploration of unconventional themes and use of modernist techniques; even its detractors noted that '*Cane* is an interesting, occasionally beautiful and often queer book of exploration into old country and new ways of writing.'[2] *Cane*'s author was equally unconventional. In 1922 Jean Toomer described himself as being the product of 'seven blood mixtures,' who had 'lived equally amid the two race groups. Now white, now coloured' and throughout his life had 'striven for a spiritual fusion analogous to the fact of racial intermingling.'[3] As *Cane*'s editors have

---

1 Nellie Y. McKay, *Jean Toomer, Artist: A Study of His Literary Life and Work, 1894–1936* (Chapel Hill and London: The University of North Carolina Press, 1984), p. ix.
2 Robert Littell, 'A Review of *Cane*' (1923), reprinted in Jean Toomer, *Cane*, second edition, edited by Rudolph P. Byrd and Henry Louis Gates Jr (New York & London: W. W. Norton, 2011), p. 183.
3 *A Jean Toomer Reader: Selected Unpublished Writings*, edited by Frederik L. Rusch (New York & Oxford: Oxford University Press, 1993), pp. 15–16.

written of the work and the man:

> Raised as an African American but, to most observers, racially
> indeterminate, Toomer embodied in his person, in his disposi-
> tion, and in his art many of the signal elements—hybridity, alien-
> ation, fragmentation, dislocation, migration, fluidity, experimen-
> tation—that define American modernism, and that he would so
> imaginatively address in *Cane*.[1]

However, even as *Cane* went into print its author's interests were
already shifting from artistic creation to the teachings of the
Armenian spiritual leader and mystic George Gurdjieff, as Toomer
began the first of a series of quests for a different kind of 'spiritual
fusion' versions of which would occupy him for the rest of his life.
These quests would take him out of the world of literature, out of
his adopted 'race group,' and into a relatively reclusive search for
forms of 'higher consciousness' which produced only didactic and
moralising writings—the antithesis of *Cane* both stylistically and
thematically—and which, for the most part, remained unpublished
during Toomer's lifetime.

The removal of its creator from the literary scene is one of the
reasons that the history of *Cane*'s production and reception is a
chequered one. In 1923 it appeared in a very small print run. It was
reprinted in 1927, but then faded from view until it was rediscovered
by scholars of African-American writing and republished in 1967—
the year that its author died in obscurity.[2] But *Cane* didn't disappear
from the literary landscape because of unfavourable reviews. Indeed,
even after the apparent disappearance of its author it acquired a 'classic' status among the period's writers and intellectuals. As the authors
of the first full-length study of Toomer wrote:

> *Cane* became one of those classics kept alive by word of mouth
> and sheer admiration on the part of its readership. This is a ver-
> ifiable statement since, when it became time for those success-
> ful figures of the 1920s to write their memoirs, *Cane* is men-
> tioned time after time as one book which stuck in the mind as

1   Byrd and Gates, 'Song of the Son', in Jean Toomer, *Cane*, second edition, p. lviii.
2   Byrd and Gates, 'Song of the Son', pp. xx–iii.

an inspirational work.[1]

Paradoxically, many of the 'problems' that *Cane* and its author faced were due to the fact that the writer and the work so successfully embodied and expressed some of the tensions and contradictions of the period that produced them. As has been suggested, the novel was an experimental work and, like Toomer himself, it was hard to categorise—and the work and its author still continue to evade easy or comfortable assessments and readings. Indeed, *Cane* charts and embodies the related tensions and complexities of not one but two movements—the Harlem Renaissance and literary modernism. The ambiguities and seeming oddities of Toomer's text constantly remind the reader that modernist scepticism, the contradictions of American racial politics, and the questioning of established ideological and artistic forms, are what make *Cane* such a troubled and fascinating work. Exploring some of the difficulties that the artist and work embody will help to open up a discussion of the conflicts that *Cane* dramatises, a book that novelist Alice Walker alleged 'sang naturally and effortlessly of the beauty, passion, and vulnerability' of black experience, while also expressing the 'divided life' of its author and his world.[2]

---

1   Brian Joseph Benson and Mabel Mayle Dillard, *Jean Toomer* (Boston: Twayne Publishers, 1980), p. 50.
2   Alice Walker, *In Search of Our Mothers' Gardens* (London: The Women's Press, 1984), p. 60.

2. Jean Toomer, the Harlem Renaissance and an Unpopular Masterpiece

2.1 The Harlem Renaissance

In the short space of time between the end of World War I and the economic decline of the Depression in the 1930s, the New York district of Harlem had formed the geographic and symbolic centre of a cultural renaissance which saw a flowering of black American expression in the arts—literary, musical, dramatic, visual—movements which can themselves be seen as signs of historical transformations in the self-awareness and political commitment of black communities which would spread out into the Western world at large. Self-confidence, critical engagement and the bid for self-realisation characterise the voices of the Harlem Renaissance, but the messages these voices carried were far from unanimously optimistic—in part because at the core of the Renaissance was a mindfulness of American history. The decades since the emancipation of the slaves in the 1860s were characterised by failures and betrayals where black Americans were systematically denied the rights, advantages and economic opportunities that their newly acquired citizenship supposedly conferred. In the South they were constrained to live under what became known as the Jim Crow laws of racial segregation, and the threat of a lynch law which made conditions, for many, worse than before the era of Reconstruction, which followed the defeat of the south in the civil war and supposedly guaranteed civil rights for ex-slaves. Social and economic experiences differed from place to place, but in varying degrees the sense of an emancipation that left a people unfree, of opportunities that were often thwarted by circumstance, and of a promise of self-realisation negated by the persistence of entrenched and destructive stereotypes, persisted. These are the circumstances and experiences that would lead W. E. B du Bois to argue in *The*

Souls of Black Folk (1903), his classic analysis of the condition of black Americans at the beginning of the twentieth century, that they laboured under a split or dual selfhood:

> After the Egyptian and the Indian, the Greek and Roman, the Teuton and Mongolian, the Negro is a sort of seventh son, born with a veil, and gifted with second-sight in this American world—a world which yields him no true self-consciousness, but only lets him see himself through the revelation of the other world. It is a peculiar sensation, this double-consciousness, this sense of always looking at one's self through the eyes of others, of measuring one's soul by the tape of a world that looks on in amused contempt and pity. One ever feels his two-ness,—an American, a Negro; two souls, two thoughts, two unreconciled strivings; two warring ideals in one dark body, whose dogged strength alone keeps it from being torn asunder.
>
> The history of the American Negro is the history of this strife—this longing to attain self-conscious manhood, to merge his double self into a better and truer self.[1]

Arguably, it is the range of artistic attempts to deal with such tensions and dualities which make the products of the Harlem Renaissance so rich, so beautiful, and often so tragic. But when we look at the movement closely two key aesthetic positions *vis-à-vis* such existential 'doubleness' emerge: one of them urges the merging of the double or split self into 'a better and truer self;' the other tends to document the struggle between the ideals that du Bois outlines, but questions the values of such ideals, and remains sceptical about the possibility, or even the desirability, of attaining anything so integrated as a 'true' self in modern America.

These positions and their antagonistic implications are easily discerned in the groupings of the movement's major figures. Alain Locke was one of the intellectual prime-movers of the Harlem Renaissance, and in 1925 he edited what is regarded as its definitive anthology, *The New Negro*. His introductory essays stress the idea that the aims and destiny of the 'new negro' coincide with the ideals of modern America:

---

1   W. E. B. Du Bois, *The Souls of Black Folk* (Harmondsworth: Penguin, 1996), p. 5.

The Negro today is inevitably moving forward under the control largely of his own objectives. What are these objectives? Those of his outer life are happily already well and finally formulated, for they are none other than the ideals of American institutions and democracy.

With these objectives ratified by the black intelligentsia of the day, Locke felt that there was a general optimism among black artists and thinkers such as those represented in *The New Negro*, who considered themselves an avant-garde, carrying a confident 'consciousness of acting as the advance-guard of the African peoples in their contact with Twentieth Century civilization.'[1] Locke's idea of an advance guard helping the African-American population assimilate and integrate themselves into 'the ideals of American institutions and democracy' has a good pedigree, as it looks back to the thinking of du Bois, who in 1903 had famously written of fostering the educated 'Talented Tenth' of the black population, raising 'the Best of this race that they may guide the Mass away from the contamination and death of the Worst, in their own and other races.' For du Bois as for Locke, this was a matter of raising the black population up to a cultural standard which was already there, and although it remains unspoken, this standard, this level of civilisation was essentially white American society and the values it had inherited from centuries of European culture. 'Was there ever a nation on God's fair earth civilized from the bottom upward? Never; it is, ever was and ever will be from the top downward that culture filters' du Bois had written,[2] and *The New Negro* and the prime movers of the Renaissance seemed to agree with him.

But such views would be contested the year after *The New Negro*'s publication by Langston Hughes, one of the most influential and gifted writers of the movement, whose essay 'The Negro Artist and the Racial Mountain' (1926) presented what is essentially the manifesto of the younger and more radical wing of the Harlem Renaissance. Hughes' essay opens with an exposé of the 'unspoken' assumptions

---

1 Alain Locke (ed.), *The New Negro* (New York: Touchstone Books, 1997), p. 10 and p. 14.
2 *Du Bois On Education*, edited by Eugene F. Provenzo (Walnut Creek C. A.: AltaMira Press, 2002), p. 76 and p. 80.

and values which resided in the entreaties for American assimilation, civilisation and 'betterment' in the writing of Locke and du Bois:

> One of the most promising of the young Negro poets said to me once, 'I want to be a poet—not a Negro poet,' meaning, I believe, 'I want to write like a white poet;' meaning subconsciously, 'I would like to be a white poet;' meaning behind that, 'I would like to be white.' And I was sorry the young man said that, for no great poet has ever been afraid of being himself. And I doubted then that, with his desire to run away spiritually from his race, this boy would ever be a great poet. But this is the mountain standing in the way of any true Negro art in America—this urge within the race toward whiteness, the desire to pour racial individuality into the mold of American standardization, and to be as little Negro and as much American as possible.[1]

Hughes' promotion of a self-consciously 'black' art and literature throws into relief the hidden Eurocentrism of writers like Locke and du Bois. But the essay was more than just a statement of an ideological position; it was also an insistence on a modern, honest and realistic approach to black American experience at the level of literary subject and theme. This was exemplified in *Fire!!*, an important, if short-lived, literary magazine that emerged in 1926 as a vehicle for the work of young Renaissance writers, and contained works by Langston Hughes, Zora Neale Hurston, Wallace Thurman, Arna Bontemps, Bruce Nugent, Gwendolyn Bennett, Lewis Alexander, Countee Cullen, and visual artists like Nugent and Aaron Douglas. All of these names are now considered to be among the leading lights of the Harlem Renaissance, but at the time the subject matter and approach of *Fire!!* caused outrage, dealing as it did with sexual promiscuity, prostitution, plebeian and 'low' life, homosexuality and bisexuality, interracial relationships, class antagonism and 'black' colour prejudice—accompanied by decadently modern or starkly ethnic illustrations and designs.

The younger generation of writers seemed to wilfully eschew the

---

1   Langston Hughes in David Levering Lewis (ed.), *The Portable Harlem Renaissance Reader* (Viking Penguin: New York and London, 1995), p. 91.

'uplifting', civilised and ultimately Eurocentric values espoused by
what Hughes would call the older 'midwives' of the movement, pre-
ferring to document the injustices and strivings of the masses—those
beneath both the socio-economic 'talented tenth' and the moral radar
of the 'Best of the race.' In 'The Negro Artist and the Racial Mountain'
Hughes critiques the mainstream expectations and demands of white
and black readers alike, and celebrates the fact that the significant
black writers fail to satisfy either group. It is noteworthy, though, that
the artist Hughes uses as his prime example of resistance to mainstream acceptance and assimilation is Jean Toomer, and the exemplary misunderstood work is *Cane*:

> The Negro artist works against an undertow of sharp criticism and
> misunderstanding from his own group and unintentional bribes
> from the whites. 'Oh, be respectable, write about nice people,
> show how good we are,' say the Negroes. 'Be stereotyped, don't
> go too far, don't shatter our illusions about you, don't amuse us
> too seriously. We will pay you,' say the whites. Both would have
> told Jean Toomer not to write *Cane*. The colored people did not
> praise it. The white people did not buy it. Most of the colored
> people who did read *Cane* hate it. They are afraid of it. Although
> the critics gave it good reviews the public remained indifferent.
> Yet (excepting the work of Du Bois) *Cane* contains the finest
> prose written by a Negro in America. And like the singing of
> Robeson, it is truly racial.[1]

I will return to the last points Hughes makes shortly, but first I
would like to refer back to the initial point made at the start of this
introduction: *Cane* didn't sell well when it was first published. Despite
the fact that Toomer didn't appear in *Fire!!* and extracts from *Cane*
were given a prominent place in *The New Negro*, Hughes can adopt
Toomer for the more radical and—at the time more unpopular—wing
of the Harlem movement. As we shall see, this was possible because
Cane's depictions of raw folk culture, its critiques of middle-class
values, and its refusal to diminish the disturbing and often horrific
elements of the characters and situations it presents, align him with

---

1   *The Portable Harlem Renaissance Reader*, p. 94.

the younger generation of writers who refused what they saw as the facile optimism of 'respectable' subjects and 'positive' racial representations.

Cane's synthesis of realism and pessimism partially accounts for the work's unpopularity and 'difficulty;' but other factors come into play here too. Toomer's novel was published 1923, and if there had been an *annus mirabilis* which set the tone of literary modernism, it was 1922, the year that preceded *Cane*'s appearance. As Kevin Jackson has noted, 1922 began with the publication of James Joyce's *Ulysses*, and closed with the publication of T. S. Eliot's *The Waste Land*—possibly the most influential English-language novel and poem of the century respectively.[1] Just weeks after *The Waste Land* appeared in print in America, Toomer would write to his friend and literary mentor Waldo Frank that 'The book is done,'[2] and although it would take almost a year for the final version of *Cane* to appear in print, it was completely at home on the stage of artistic innovation which other works had set for it, and would itself be regarded almost immediately as a landmark of American experimental modernism.

2.2 Modernism and Folk Songs

Cane's modernist character is apparent in its generic mix of poetry, prose and drama, and in its essentially fragmented tripartite structure. This structure traces a route through time and space from the agrarian timelessness of the American south, through to the brash urban modernity of the northern city, to return, rootless and dissatisfied, to the modern but underdeveloped south. In 'The South in Literature,' an anonymous and unpublished review of *Cane* and his friend Waldo Frank's novel *Holiday*, which were both published at the same time by Boni and Liveright, Toomer gives an outline of his own work's shape and themes which is worth quoting at length.

Cane is a collection of poems, short stories, and one long drama,

---

1 Kevin Jackson, *Constellation of Genius 1922: Modernism Year One* (London: Hutchinson, 2012), p. 2.
2 *Brother Mine: The Correspondence of Jean Toomer and Waldo Frank*, edited by Kathleen Pfeiffer (Urbana: University of Illinois Press, 2010), p. 85.

all of which are notable for their lyricism and evocation of the Southern atmosphere. There are three sub-divisions of the book.

The materials of Part One are those of middle Georgia. Poems and short story themes arise from a symphony of red soil, pine trees, cane-brakes and cotton fields, swamps, saw-mills, old Negro cabins, and hills and valleys saturate with the blood and toil, the songs and sufferings of the slave regime. The themes themselves weave about young Negro girls whose dusky loveliness flowers for a moment, yields to the insistent claims of love, then fades, as all natural beauty must ...

In Part Two the milieu shifts to Washington, but it is still Southern and still Negro. Here, however, the slow peasant rhythm, the peasant's basic adjustment to his physical environment give way to more strident cadences. And the life becomes more conscious, more restless and stirring, and hence more complex ....

Part Three, a single drama, swings back to middle Georgia. Here again one finds the hills and valleys resonant with folk songs, saturate with the pain and joy, the ugliness and beauty of a peasant people. The elemental pulse of these, together with the impalpable fog of white dominance and its implications which the raw sensibility of Ralph Kabnis (the protagonist) spreads over the entire countryside, are too strong and oppressive for his depleted sensibilities to grapple with.[1]

This self-description affords a good overview of Toomer's novel, but it doesn't do justice to its own modernist features and innovations. The 'lyricism and evocation' of the prose treatment of the south is mentioned here, but what isn't emphasised is the way in which Toomer's writing splices poetry and prose together in sustained ways throughout, achieving an image-rich prose poetry and a distinctive style which he himself would describe as 'poetic realist.'[2] Add to this the novel's discontinuous and fragmented narrative passages,

1   *Jean Toomer: Selected Essays and Literary Criticism*, edited by Robert B. Jones (Knoxville: The University of Tennessee Press, 1996), pp. 14–15.
2   Jean Toomer, *The Wayward and the Seeking: A Collection of Writings by Jean Toomer*, edited by Darwin W. Turner (Washington D. C.: Howard University Press, 1982), p. 20.

the montage effects that generic mixing and intertextual references and allusions create, the imagist cast of much of the poetry, and the extensive use of interior monologue, and this amounts to a text as dense and difficult in its way as the modernist experiments of Joyce and Eliot.

Such radically new features add to the kind of resistance to popular consumption that *Cane*'s poor sales figures testify to. But the other side of these innovative and unfamiliar modernist forms is the lyrical, nostalgic invocation of the black experience of the south through a 'symphony of red soil, pine trees, cane-brakes and cotton fields' which the novel contains. When Langston Hughes wrote that '*Cane* contains the finest prose written by a Negro in America,' and proclaimed that 'like the singing of Robeson, it is truly racial,' he was alluding to the recurring fragments of gospel or spiritual song lyrics which punctuate and often frame the prose sections of Cane. The singer Paul Robeson was famous for his repertoire of spirituals, those distinctive song forms which had emerged, like the blues and jazz would emerge later, from the nearest thing to a rural peasantry that America had: the black American slave class of the southern states. Robeson and others had essentially given a voice to black American folk experience, and, in the absence of a written history of their own, this folk music became communal testimony of the yearning for emancipation, and an oral vehicle for the history of black Americans. This is the 'racial' quality that Hughes discerns in Toomer's writing and Robeson's voice, for, as du Bois had written in *The Souls of Black Folk* of what he called 'The Sorrow Songs' of the south, they were evidence of a black history, identity and rootedness in the soil of the south:

> They that walked in darkness sang songs in the olden days—
> Sorrow Songs—for they were weary at heart ... these weird old
> songs in which the soul of the black slave spoke to men. Ever
> since I was a child these songs have stirred me strangely. They
> came out of the South unknown to me, one by one, and yet at once
> I knew them as of me and of mine ... Out of them rose for me
> morning, noon, and night, bursts of wonderful melody, full of the

voices of my brothers and sisters, full of the voices of the past.[1]

In such songs and music du Bois—like many after him—heard the echoes of remembered African traditions, sublimated field hollers and shouts from the days of slavery, transmogrified European hymns and traditions that had evolved into distinctly black American expressions which contained 'the siftings of centuries,'[2] preserving the voice of black experience as it had defied the passage and violence of history. The folk songs mean the same for Toomer as they had for du Bois. Indeed, despite the fact that Toomer's racial identity was, as we shall see, in a state of renegotiation after the publication of *Cane*, in a letter of April 1923 he suggested the rhythms of the sorrow songs did nothing less than affirm his identity: 'In so far as the old folk-songs, syncopated rhythms, the rich sweet taste of dark-skinned life, in so far as these are Negro, I am, body and soul, Negroid.'[3] True to form, however, Toomer's text does not simply enshrine or celebrate the songs and lyrics that it contains. In *Cane* the spirituals, and the history of experience they encapsulate, are cherished for their tragic beauty and significance, yet, as one of Toomer's most cited autobiographical statements about his work makes clear, he considers them to be doomed to disappear in the noise and progress of modernity:

> There was a valley, the valley of 'Cane,' with smoke-wreaths during the day and mist at night. A family of back-country Negroes had only recently moved into a shack not too far away. They sang. And this was the first time I'd ever heard the folk-songs and spirituals. They were sad and joyous and beautiful. But I learned that the Negroes of the town objected to them. They called them 'shouting.' They had victrolas and player-pianos. So, I realized with deep regret, that the spirituals, meeting ridicule, would be certain to die out. With Negroes also the trend was towards the small town and then towards the city—and industry and commerce and machines. The folk-spirit was walking in to die on the modern desert. The spirit was so beautiful. Its death

---

1   *The Souls of Black Folk*, pp. 204–5.
2   *The Souls of Black Folk*, p. 207.
3   *The Letters of Jean Toomer 1919–1924*, edited by Mark Whalan (Knoxville: University of Tennessee Press, 2006), p. 160.

was so tragic. Just this seemed to sum life for me. And this was the feeling I put into *Cane*. *Cane* was a swan-song. It was a song of an end. And why no one has seen and felt that, why people have expected me to write a second and a third and a fourth book like *Cane*, is one of the queer misunderstandings of my life.[1]

Here, Toomer is referring to the three months he spent in the fall of 1921 as the acting principal of the Sparta Agricultural and Industrial Institute in Georgia. After years of odd jobs and uncompleted college courses, he had jumped at this post as a break from caring for his ageing grandparents in Washington, and a source of income. But he got more than he bargained for. As his autobiographical writings suggest, his sojourn in Sparta was his first exposure to the south, the black culture that it contained and the ancestral history that its people and landscape seemed to offer to him.[2] Here was a culture, cemented by religious faith, song, shared hardship and deep feeling, that had upheld and sustained a people for generations, and here Toomer found the inspiration for *Cane* and the lyrical evocation of the south for which his text is so valued. He began writing the sketches for the first section of *Cane* on the train as he returned to Washington. However, as Toomer maintains, this evocation of the south is one of the most 'misunderstood' aspects of his writing—or rather the paucity of it— since the publication of the novel in 1923. Attempting to understand exactly why he regarded these aspects of his novel as 'a swan-song ... a song of an end,' or the coda of a period of transition, will help us to examine the most controversial facet of Toomer's thinking and writing—his attitude towards race.

2.3 Toomer and Race

Jean Toomer was born in 1894, into a family whose racial indeterminacy—or what he would call 'racial intermingling'— stretched back over several generations. His father, Nathan Toomer

---

1   *The Wayward and the Seeking*, p. 123.
2   It was also a town where his father had lived; see Robert B. Jones, *Jean Toomer and the Prison-house of Thought: A Phenomenology of the Spirit* (Amherst: University of Massachusetts Press, 1993), p. 28.

was born a slave, being the son of a Georgia planter of European extraction and a slave woman of mixed race.[1] His mother, Nina Pinchback, was the daughter of Pinckney Benton Stewart (P.B.S.) Pinchback , who was himself the son of Major William Pinchback, a Virginia plantation owner, and Eliza Stewart, a mixed race woman from New Orleans. Nina's mother was Emily Hethorne, an Anglo-French woman of mixed race. Jean's grandfather P. B. S. Pinchback had been given a good education because the conventions of the south dictated that wealthy plantation owners raised their illegitimate 'mulatto' offspring as well as their financial standing would allow. Although Pinchback's family fell on hard times after the Major's death, P. B. S. Pinchback would rise to prominence and become 'the first African American to serve as governor of a state when he was appointed in 1872 as acting governor of Louisiana.'[2] Toomer's father abandoned the family when Jean was a year old, and despite the decline of grandfather Pinchback's political and economic fortunes, Jean would live with his mother and grandparents in a range of domestic arrangements and social environments until well into adulthood. He initially lived with his mother and grandparents in a middle-class district of Washington D. C. His mother remarried in 1906 and Toomer lived with them in different New York neighbourhoods until his mother's death in 1909, when he moved back to live with his grandparents in different areas of Washington.

Jean Toomer's mixed racial heritage meant that he inhabited a hybridised terrain which revealed the segregationist 'color-line'—which du Bois had defined as 'the problem of the Twentieth Century'—to be the crude and arbitrary division that it was.[3] Toomer's ancestry, and his family's uneven fortunes and relocations, determined that he had lived in both white and black, segregated and mixed, affluent and poor environments during his formative years. In some ways the visit to Georgia and his experiences there seemed to 'complete'

1   Byrd and Gates, 'Song of the Son', in *Cane*, second edition, p. xxvi.
2   Werner Sollers, 'Jean Toomer's *Cane*: Modernism and Race in Interwar America,' in Geneviève Fabre and Michael Feith (eds) *Jean Toomer and the Harlem Renaissance* (New Jersey and London: Rutgers University Press, 2001),.pp. 18–37.
3   Du Bois, *The Souls of Black Folks*, p. 1.

an aspect of Toomer's identity that allowed him a sense of 'racial' belonging and community for the first time. It also allowed him the creative inspiration that gave rise to *Cane*. In a letter of 1922 which was briefly cited at the opening of this chapter Toomer would write:

> Racially, I seem to have (who knows for sure) seven blood mixtures: French, Dutch, Welsh, Negro, German, Jewish, and Indian. Because of these, my position in America has been a curious one. I have lived equally amid the two race groups. Now white, now colored. From my own point of view I am naturally and inevitably an American. I have strived for a spiritual fusion analogous to the fact of racial intermingling. Without denying a single element in me, with no desire to subdue one to the other, I have sought to let them function as complements. I have tried to let them live in harmony. Within the last two or three years, however, my growing need for artistic expression has pulled me deeper and deeper into the Negro group. And as my powers of receptivity increased, I found myself loving it in a way that I could never love the other. It has stimulated and fertilized whatever creative talent I may contain within me. A visit to Georgia last fall was the starting point of almost everything of worth that I have done. I heard folk-songs come from the lips of Negro peasants. I saw the rich dusk beauty that I had heard many false accents about, and of which till then, I was somewhat skeptical. And a deep part of my nature, a part that I had repressed, sprang suddenly to life and responded to them.[1]

Even here, Toomer prefaces his remarks about his 'deep' response to the south with an insistence that 'From my own point of view I am naturally and inevitably an American,' and even before the publication of *Cane*, he would insist that what he had captured in art was the passing of an era. Essentially, even as *Cane* was at the printers, Toomer came to consider it as the passing of a cultural epoch in which the racial category of the Negro had any meaning. As he wrote to Waldo Frank shortly before the novel was published:

> There is one thing about the Negro in America which the most

---

1   *A Jean Toomer Reader*, pp. 15–16.

> thoughtful persons seem to ignore: the Negro is in solution, in
> the process of solution. As an entity, the race is loosing [*sic*]
> its body, and its soul is approaching a common soul ... Don't
> let us fool ourselves, brother: the Negro of the folk-song has
> all but passed away: the Negro of the emotional church is
> fading. A hundred years from now these Negroes, if they exist
> at all will be in art.[1]

Controversially, Toomer would come to object to being labelled as
'negro' in the introduction to his work (it would be a factor in his
estrangement from his friend Waldo Frank, who had supplied the
introductory essay for *Cane*) and would respond angrily to his publisher's suggestion that he was 'evading' his African-American identity in resisting the label 'negro' in the biographical publicity that pro-
moted the book, insisting that 'My racial composition and my position
in the world are realities which I alone may determine.'[2] Once again,
there are several ways of approaching and assessing Toomer's position here. On one hand, his vision is futuristic and utopian: he seemed
to consider *Cane* as his first and final word on a southern culture
which modernity was sweeping away, and rather than lament its loss,
he saw it as an inevitable, if unfortunate, effect of progress. Similarly,
his insistence that he was 'naturally and inevitably an American' can
be regarded as a refusal to fall into the outmoded pseudo-scientific
discourse of race, with its reifying logic of bifurcation, hierarchy and
persecution.[3] In the 1920s and 1930s, when both Europe and America
were awash with racial and racist ideologies, Toomer was pleading
intelligently against discourses of biological essentialism and racial
categorisation:

> ... it is a mistake to speak of blood as if it had various colors in
> the various human races. All human blood is the same. When we
> use color adjectives what we really are referring to are skin pig-

---

1   *Brother Mine: The Correspondence of Jean Toomer and Waldo Frank*, p. 101.
2   *A Jean Toomer Reader*, p. 94.
3   On Toomer's resistance to 'racial reification,' or the transformation of the abstract
    fictions of race into biological fact and social segregation, see Robert B. Jones,
    Jean Toomer and the Prison-house of Thought, pp. 4–7.

mentations. This is one of our main troubles. We see a surface and assume it is a center. We see a color or a label or a picture and assume it is a person …

There is only one pure race—and that is the human race. We all belong to it—and this is the most and the least that can be said for us with accuracy. For the rest, it is mere talk, mere labelling….[1]

In 1923, however, Toomer was protesting against a more imminent and domestic system of racial exclusion and oppression. In the early years of the twentieth century the white population were reacting in increasingly hostile ways against the slow rise of a black bourgeois professional class, and a lot of social and political measures were being taken to define and preserve the distinction between the 'races' which, since the end of slavery, had become increasingly blurred. The most effective way that this bifurcation was imposed was through the 'one drop' rule—in which any trace of mixed ancestry or 'negro' blood meant than an individual became racially categorised as 'black'—which became increasingly adopted as law under Woodrow Wilson's presidency. Beneath such attitudes and laws, Toomer and his family, and all like him, were being rendered invisible. As George Hutchinson writes:

> Perhaps the greatest irony of Toomer's career is that at the time modern American racial discourse was taking its most definite shape, 'mulattoes'—because they threatened the racial bifurcation—'disappeared' as a group into either the white 'race' (through passing) or the black 'race' while the 'one drop rule' was defined in increasingly definite terms. The 1920 census, coinciding with the beginning of the Harlem Renaissance, was the last to count 'mulattoes.' At the same time, 'interracial' mating, and particularly 'interracial' marriage, rare as it already was, drastically declined.[2]

---

1 *A Jean Toomer Reader: Selected Unpublished Writings*, p. 109.
2 George Hutchinson, 'Jean Toomer and American Racial Discourse,' *Texas Studies in Literature and Language*, 35: 2 (Summer 1993), pp. 226–50, p. 229.

Hutchinson points out elsewhere that this period of black / white 'polarisation' of American racial discourse occurred during the course of Toomer's life, and that ultimately 'The United States would be more segregated at the time of Toomer's death than it had been at the time of his birth, despite the dismantling of some of the legal bulwarks of white supremacy.'[1]

When such factors are taken into account, it must be appreciated that there are deep historical, political, social and personal reasons behind Toomer's insistence that he was 'naturally and inevitably an American.' And also historical, political and social reasons behind his failure to be allowed to inhabit any space outside of this racial discourse apart from through 'passing' as white or accepting categorisation as black. His urge to transcend the dehumanising constraints of racial categorisation have been summed up by his biographers:

> Thus Toomer propounded the rather unpopular view that the racial issue in America would be resolved only when white America could accept the fact that its racial "purity" was a myth … On the other hand, racial purity among blacks was just as much a myth and only encouraged defensiveness and unconscious imitation … Race, he said, was a fictional construct, of no use for understanding people ….[2]

The idea that this position was 'rather unpopular' is an understatement, and he withdrew from the world of American letters as his stance on race became increasingly misunderstood. After the publication of *Cane*, Toomer became a follower of Gurdjieff, the first figure in a series of spiritual leaders and disciplines that allowed him to pursue a quest for spiritual wholeness and turn his back on literature. Perhaps it is the case that Toomer became convinced that his writing had just locked him more firmly in the racist ideologies and linguistic systems that he was trying to circumvent. Alice Walker has insisted that after *Cane*, Toomer's life and work offered little for those seeking any

---

1   George Hutchinson, 'Identity in Motion: Placing *Cane,*' in Fabre and Fleiss (eds), *Jean Toomer and the Harlem Renaissance*, pp. 38–56, pp. 53–54.

2   Cynthia Earl Kerman and Richard Eldridge, *The Lives of Jean Toomer: A Hunger for Wholeness* (Baton Rouge and London: Louisiana State University Press, 1987), p. 342.

treatment of black American experience:

> ... because the man who wrote so piercingly of 'Negro' life in
> *Cane* chose to live his own life as a white man, while Hughes,
> Hurston, Du Bois and other black writers were celebrating the
> blackness in themselves as well as in their work.[1]

Quite whether Walker's judgement is accurate here is debateable, but
it is possible to sympathise with her position and at the same time
appreciate why Toomer, the man of mixed race who was driven by
the urge to eliminate the binary and exclusivist logic of race, couldn't
produce a work that merely celebrated or affirmed a particular
identity, group of people or aspect of historical experience. Now
we are perhaps in a better position to see how *Cane*'s treatment of
'alienation, fragmentation, dislocation' has an integrity and sincerity
that gives it a special place in modern literature, and we can return
to the contradictions and tensions of Toomer's text to get a truthful
picture of his experience, and a clearer sense of his world as the
portent of our own.

---

1   Walker, *In Search of Our Mother's Gardens*, p. 62.

3 Literary Influences and Strategies

3.1 Early Influences

Jean Toomer grew up fatherless in a family dominated by a maternal grandfather who was a public figure, and P. B. S. Pinchback maintained a firm patriarchal hold over his household even as his fortunes declined. In this environment Toomer found himself searching for a more sympathetic father figure, and he eventually found one in his uncle Bismarck:

> Uncle Bis and I suddenly discovered each other. He had been there all along and his sensitivity and affection had drawn me to him ....
>
> He had a habit—but it was more than a habit; it was a passion—of coming home from work, having dinner with the family, and immediately retiring to his room. There he would get in bed with a book, cigarettes, and a saucer of sliced peaches ... and read far into the night ....
>
> This position—my uncle in bed surrounded by the materials of a literary man—was impressed upon me as one of the desirable positions in life. It is no wonder that later on I responded positively to pictures of Robert Louis Stevenson and other writers spending most of their lives in bed. Nor is it surprising that in time I inclined to a career which would let me live this way if I wanted to.[1]

The rather decadent role-model of Uncle Bismarck provided an effective bohemian foil to his grandfather's strictness, and for the remainder of Toomer's life his relationship with his grandfather would be strained as a result of Pinchbeck's disapproval of the

---

1 Toomer, *The Wayward and the Seeking*, pp. 41–2.

apparently noncommittal artistic lifestyle that his grandson had chosen for himself.

What Uncle Bismarck actually provided for Toomer was an education in literature, science and ideas that the boy had failed to get at any of the schools he attended. Indeed, Toomer's schooling was uneven. He had difficulty with application, concentration and reading, and when he forced himself to read he found none of the stories 'half as wonderful as those told me by Bismarck.'[1] Biographers and critics have speculated that family moves and conflicts between his social and educational lives caused by his ethnic background added to Toomer's educational problems: he lived in a predominantly white Washington neighbourhood but attended a 'coloured' school; after his mother's marriage he attended a white school in New York, but lived in a 'coloured' area and attended a segregated school on his return to Washington after his mother's death.[2] But this resistance to formal education, or a resistance to persevering with a course of schooling after a certain level of interest had been satisfied, continued throughout Toomer's early manhood. After graduating from high school, Toomer went on to study at university level, taking courses in history, sociology, scientific agriculture, physical training, law, socialism and, strangely, atheism; finally, he 'matriculated at six colleges and universities between 1914 and 1918,' but ultimately 'failed to earn a degree.'[3]

During these years Toomer continued his own patterns of reading, discovering the works of George Bernard Shaw, Walt Whitman, and Goethe—whose *Wilhelm Meister* (1796) seemed to have the effect, like the work of several other writers and thinkers throughout Toomer's life, of providing him with an identity and a destiny. Goethe's tale of self-realisation through art, Toomer would write,

> ... seemed to gather together all the scattered parts of myself. I was lifted into and shown my real world. It was the world of the aristocrat—but not the social aristocrat; the aristocrat of culture,

---

1   *The Wayward and the Seeking*, p. 46.
2   Byrd and Gates, 'Song of the Son' in *Cane* (second edition), pp. xxxii–xxxiv; Kerman and Eldridge, *The Lives of Jean Toomer*, p. 36.
3   Byrd and Gates, 'Song of the Son', p. xli.

of spirit and character, of ideas, of true nobility. And for the first
time in years and years I breathed the air of my own land.[1]

Despite the self-dramatisation, Toomer took this calling seriously,
moving to New York in 1918 and enrolling in the radical Rand
School where his political views developed a distinct left-wing turn.
Although Toomer played down his early political interests in his
later autobiographical writings it was at this time that he met writers
and thinkers associated with publications like *The Liberator* and
New York Call, and his first published articles (on war profiteering,
the Washington race riots of 1919, and a critique of a veiled attack
on Waldo Frank's *Our America*) appeared in the *Call* in 1919 and
1920.[2] Despite Toomer's political engagement during this period,
and an interest in atheism and socialism, his autobiographical
writings admit that a move back to Washington saw him sitting up
at night 'rediscovering' religious writings, 'Buddhist philosophy,
the Eastern teachings, occultism, theosophy,' which re-lit dormant
spiritual interests: 'My religious nature which had been sleeping,'
Toomer writes, 'was vigorously aroused.'[3] The passion of Toomer's
commitment to systems of ideas is evident in such statements and
in the wide reading that informs them; but these passions would
also drive the massive shifts in worldview which would eventually
displace his literary ambitions and replace them with spiritual ones
after the publication of *Cane*.

In the years leading up to 1920 however, *Cane* was still a project
whose multiple threads and strands were only just beginning to be
woven together, and Toomer seemed able to keep his religious and
literary interests separate—although he also read the Bible 'as literature' during this period.[4] Toomer's autobiographical writings are curiously silent about other inputs into his literary development which
took place in Washington at this time, but they were inputs that were

---

1 Toomer, *The Wayward and the Seeking*, p. 112.
2 These essays are reproduced and widely discussed in Charles Scruggs and
   Lee Vandemarr, *Jean Toomer and the Terrors of American History* (Philadelphia:
   University of Pennsylvania Press, 1998).
3 Toomer, *The Wayward and the Seeking*, p. 119 and p. 120.
4 McKay, *Jean Toomer, Artist*, p. 30.

crucial for the consolidation of his ideas of race and identity. Since early 1919 Toomer had been attending the salons of the mixed-race poet Georgia Douglas Johnson:

> Known among the cognoscenti of the nation's capital as Saturday Nighters, these gatherings attracted such luminaries of the Harlem Renaissance as Zora Neale Hurston, Richard Bruce Nugent, Sterling A. Brown, Countee Cullen, Langston Hughes, and Alain Locke.[1]

George Hutchinson has researched this period of Toomer's development and shown that the group discussed literature and aspects of African-American history including slavery and racial ideology, and that Toomer took a leading role in some of these discussions, presenting ideas and work in progress—some of which may even have been early drafts of material that would end up in *Cane*.[2] Hutchinson suggests quite plausibly that Toomer's posthumously published play *Natalie Mann* dramatizes something of the dynamics of these gatherings, dealing as it does with a multi-ethnic group of writers and intellectuals and a schism between those who value black folk culture and those who are imitative of white bourgeois culture—a tension which, as noted earlier, would be central to the Harlem Renaissance itself. In *Natalie Mann*, it is the non-repressed, rooted and spirited exponents of black folk and popular culture that the drama endorses, suggesting that even before his trip to Sparta in 1922 Toomer had an interest in 'the folk spirit' of the south, the black popular culture of the north and the vital place they should occupy in any modern black artistic movement. Of equal importance to the development of Toomer's literary and political consciousness, however, is the way in which the fact of 'racial intermingling' and the supposed miscegenation which was its source was introduced into the group—possibly by Toomer himself. Georgia Johnson was of mixed heritage, and Hutchinson cites one of the poems from her volume *Bronze* (1922) to make a point about the ways in which ideas

---

1 Byrd and Gates, 'Song of the Son', p. xlv.
2 George Hutchinson, 'Jean Toomer and the 'New Negroes' of Washington,' *American Literature* 63: 41 (December 1991); reprinted in Byrd and Gates Jr (eds), *Cane*, second edition, pp. 305–12, pp. 305–7..

that emerged from the group's thinking challenged the racial taboos of the time:

> COSMOPOLITE
> Not wholly this or that,
> But wrought
> Of alien bloods am I,
> A product of the interplay
> Of traveled hearts.
> Estranged, yet not estranged, I stand
> All comprehending;
> From my estate
> I view earth's frail dilemma;
> Scion of fused strength am I,
> All understanding,
> Nor this nor that
> Contains me.[1]

As Hutchinson notes, the 'Scion of fused strength' and the evader of repressive categories that Johnson imagines herself to be refuses the role of 'tragic mulatto' or biracial invisibility that the ideologies and conventions of the time were imposing upon its mixed race population; these ideas would, of course, become central to Toomer's later enquiries into racial identity and the synthesis that he saw as the essence of modern America.

The spirit of the Washington Saturday Nighters would help to incubate the Harlem Renaissance, but Toomer was also absorbing a range of influences from his reading of white American and Anglo-American modernism. He would write:

> This was the period when I was so strongly influenced, first, by the Americans who were dealing with local materials in a poetic way. Robert Frost's New England poems strongly appealed to me. Sherwood Anderson's *Winesburg, Ohio* opened my eyes to entirely new possibilities. I thought it was one of the finest

---

1   Cited in Hutchinson, 'Jean Toomer and the "New Negroes" of Washington,' p. 308. The poem was originally published in Georgia Douglas Camp Johnson, *Bronze: A Book of Verse* (Boston: B. J. Brimmer Company, 1922), p. 59.

books I'd ever read. And, second, the poems and program of the Imagists. Their insistence on fresh vision and on the perfect clean economical line was just what I had been looking for. I began feeling that I had in hands the tools for my own creation.[1]

The avant-garde program of the Imagists and their influence on Toomer's literary technique will be discussed shortly. What must be noted first is the inspiration he drew from American authors like Robert Frost, Sherwood Anderson and others, who were 'dealing with local materials in a poetic way' in order to realise an American cultural and national voice.

Robert Frost's dialogue and narrative poems, such as those contained in *North of Boston* (1914), present portraits of New England farm folk in idiomatic blank verse. The volume is characterised by ideas of the land, community, stoic individualism and communication—both meaningful and unsuccessful—being simply presented, often through symbolic occurrences and incidents, as in 'Mending Wall':

> Something there is that doesn't love a wall,
> That sends the frozen-ground-swell under it,
> And spills the upper boulders in the sun,
> And makes gaps even two can pass abreast ...
>
> We wear our fingers rough with handling them.
> Oh, just another kind of out-door game,
> One on a side. It comes to little more:
> There where it is we do not need the wall:
> He is all pine and I am apple orchard.
> My apple trees will never get across
> And eat the cones under his pines, I tell him.
> He only says, "'Good fences make good neighbors".[2]

As critics have shown, Toomer's writing is indebted to Frost in that it too strives to realise ways in which local speech and dialect can embody place, and shows that all too often dialogue is merely

---

1   Toomer, *The Wayward and the Seeking*, p. 120.
2   Robert Frost, *North of Boston* (Charleston: Nabu Press, 2011), pp. 11–12.

talking to oneself—or failed communication.[1] Sherwood Anderson's *Winesburg, Ohio* similarly focuses on a contemporary American locale, using a short-story cycle to present fragments of small town life, connected through theme and character but not chronologically organised. Despite the sense of community that reluctantly arises between the disparate characters in *Winesburg, Ohio*, the presiding atmosphere is of loneliness and loss, repetition and futility. Sentences overlap, terms recur, and too often the narrative details lead to a *cul-de-sac*:

> When David Hardy was a tall boy of fifteen, he, like his mother, had an adventure that changed the whole current of his life and sent him out of his quiet corner into the world. The shell of the circumstances of his life was broken and he was compelled to start forth. He left Winesburg and no one there ever saw him again. After his disappearance, his mother and grandfather both died and his father became very rich. He spent much money in trying to locate his son, but that is no part of this story.[2]

Like the modernist short stories in James Joyce's collection *Dubliners*, Anderson's tales are often narrated through the language and to some extent the point of view of the central character. Often, authorial comment is minimised, allowing the tone to leave the reader with a sense of claustrophobia and a rather grim feeling of grinding determinism (what Joyce would famously call a sense of social and psychological 'paralysis' in his own short stories) and such techniques and themes would become a feature of *Cane* too. Toomer's letters testify to how much Anderson's works had influenced him when *Cane* was in its formative stages, but a term of disapproval applied to some of Toomer's stories by the editor of a literary magazine perhaps sums up their similarity best. Toomer wrote in a letter of 1922 that he had sent some stories which would eventually find a place in *Cane* to the *Dial*, and the editor had returned them saying 'These

---

1 Karen Jackson Ford, *Split-Gut Song: Jean Toomer and the Poetics of Modernity* (Tuscaloosa: The University of Alabama Press, 2005), pp. 19–20.
2 Sherwood Anderson, *Winesburg, Ohio* (Oxford: Oxford University Press, 1997), p. 71.

manuscripts are interesting, but it seems to me, unfulfilled.'[1] A term such as 'unfulfilled' can be applied to many modernist short stories as a label which fits one of the genre's central and intended effects, and the sense of incompletion, disenchantment and 'paralysis' in their modernist senses certainly permeates Anderson's short stories, and will, as we shall see, be key features in Toomer's work.

3.2 Waldo Frank

In August 1920, after attending a lecture on the French writer Romain Rolland and his 10-volume novel *Jean-Christophe* (1904–12) given by Helena DeKay at the Rand School, Toomer was motivated to change his own name to Jean (but pronounced as a contraction of his second name, Eugene) in admiration of the novel's eponymous musician-artist-outsider. The lecture also inspired Toomer to take up music for a period—but of more immediate significance is that, after introducing himself to DeKay he was taken to a party hosted by the author Lola Ridge, future editor of the avant-garde magazine *Broom*, where he met a group of intellectuals and writers, including the American author who would become both a major influence and the literary midwife of *Cane*, Waldo Frank.[2]

Despite his relative obscurity now, at the time of their first acquaintance Waldo Frank was 'one of the prime forces in American literary and cultural life.'[3] After their first meeting Toomer had gone on to defend Frank's *Our America* (1919) against criticism in his third *Call* article (October 1920). Frank wrote to thank Toomer for his defence, but it wasn't until 1922, after Toomer's experiences in Sparta, that a period of unbroken correspondence began which would help usher *Cane* into the world. Toomer's first letter to Frank asks about the omission of the black American experience from *Our America*, Frank's extended manifesto which called on modern artists to begin a process of visionary cultural regeneration:

---

1 *Brother Mine: The Correspondence of Jean Toomer and Waldo Frank*, p. 50.
2 Scruggs and Vandemarr, *Jean Toomer and the Terrors of American History*, pp. 61–2.
3 Kerman and Eldridge, *The Lives of Jean Toomer*, p. 86.

In your Our America I missed your not including the Negro.
I have often wondered about it. My own life has been about
equally divided between the two racial groups. My grandfather,
owing to his emphasis upon a fraction of Negro blood in his
veins, attained prominence in Reconstruction politics. And the
family, for the most part, ever since, has lived between the two
worlds, now dipping into the Negro, now into the white. Some
few are definitely white; others definitely colored. I alone have
stood for a synthesis in the matters of the mind and spirit analogous, perhaps, to the actual fact of at least six blood minglings.
The history, traditions, and culture of five of these are available
in some approximation to the truth. Of the Negro, what facts are
known have too often been perverted for the purposes of propa-
ganda, one way or the other. It has been necessary, therefore, that
I spend a disproportionate time in Negro study.[1]

Frank immediately made steps to rectify this omission, in part through
a close friendship with Toomer which quickly became intimate and
intense on both sides. In late 1922 both men would travel to the south
as black men—Frank was Jewish but dark-skinned and passed as
'coloured'—in order to further their respective researches into a new
American literature, and, right up until the rupture in their friendship
at the end of 1923,[2] Frank would promote Toomer's work and try to
provide him with opportunities for work and financial relief.

   One thing that was central to their friendship was a shared sense
of artistic mission which Frank's *Our America* had helped define for
Toomer and for the coterie of writers that he would introduce the
younger author to—through correspondence if not in person—which
included Sherwood Anderson, Carl Sandburg, and Hart Crane, as
well as critics like Gorham Munson, Lola Ridge, John McClure and
Kenneth Burke. Frank's *Our America* had looked to the 'margins' of
the American nation and an artistic vanguard in order to anticipate
an awakening, 'the best expression of Our America' which its writers could achieve;[3] a modern American cultural voice which could

---

1   *Brother Mine: The Correspondence of Jean Toomer and Waldo Frank*, p. 28.
2   Caused, in part, by Toomer's affair with Frank's wife.
3   Waldo Frank, *Our America* (New York: Boni and Liveright, 1919), p. 7.

displace the hegemonic hold of European values. According to *Our America*: 'The European cultures, swept to America and there buried, were half-killed by the mere uprooting. They were never American: they could never live *in* America. The principle of death carried them from Europe.'[1] Accordingly, Frank's prophetic manifesto extols the potential artistic renaissance that the Native American, the Mexican and Latin American, the Jewish and the new 'young' classes and artists emerging from the metropolitan cities might realise in what the title of chapter IV calls 'The Land of Buried Cultures.' As Toomer noted, the culture of the African American was missing from this list, but this is hardly surprising, as even the anthropologists and ethnographers who were scouring America for vanishing native cultures in the early twentieth century ignored black experience. At the time that early Native American rituals were being recorded for prosperity, it was mainly the nostalgic memories of ageing white plantation families, and their recollections of songs their slaves and nannies taught them, that were standing in for the black American voice. African Americans, because of their experiences of deracination, diaspora and supposed assimilation, weren't deemed to have a culture of their own.[2] Frank immediately perceived this lack and adopted Toomer as a connection to a buried culture that *Our America* had missed— and his idealised vision of America needed all of the 'marginalised' cultures that it could marshal, appearing as it did at a time of rising American anti-Semitism, which also coincided with the regressive racial categorisation and invisibility of the 'mulatto' that Toomer saw contemporary political and legal discourses enacting.[3]

Our America culminates with the giant figure of Walt Whitman, who is exalted as the prophet of the modern nation:

> The one true hierarchy of values in the world is the hierarchy of Consciousness. Most men stir about upon their little plane and know it badly … But there are souls whose consciousness

---

1 Frank, *Our America*, p. 106.
2 See for example Marybeth Hamilton, *In Search of the Blues* (New York: Basic Books, 2008), chapter 3.
3 See Scruggs and Vandemarr, *Jean Toomer and the Terrors of American History*, pp. 85–100.

is higher ….

> These are the great mystics. Such a one was Whitman. He saw
> the movements of men upon the flat plains of human life in its
> relation to all mundane life. He saw the unitary flow of all mun-
> dane life in its relation to an infinite Being of which it was an
> elementary part.[1]

The gift of special vision, a higher order of consciousness, and an
ability to represent the interpenetration of the mundane and the
'infinite' are all gifts which Frank detected in Whitman, and that
Frank and Toomer, using the critical vocabulary of the day, would
themselves see as the true 'mystical' goals of artistic aspiration.
Despite the cabalistic overtones, however, *Our America* would be
pragmatic in its hopes for modern American culture. It venerated
the new avant-garde groupings that had emerged around the New
York photographer and gallery owner Alfred Stieglitz, saying that on
entering his influential gallery 'You were in a church consecrate to
them who had lost old gods, and whose need was sore for new ones.'[2]
At the other end of the cultural spectrum, however, Frank eulogised
Charlie Chaplin as 'our most significant and most authentic dramatic
figure,'[3] regarding his democratic productions as part of an organic
popular theatre. Such a collocation of avant-garde and popular
impulses was crucial for Frank's vision of American cultural renewal,
and as we shall see, such juxtapositions and connections comprised
the core of Toomer's literary strategies in *Cane*.

3.3 Imagism

These strategies start before the reader turns to the first page of *Cane*,
for the work is prefaced by texts and images which act as an overture.
On the title page there is a block of italicised free verse containing
images which will recur throughout the book like leitmotifs:

---

1   Frank, *Our America*, p. 202.
2   Frank, *Our America*, p. 184.
3   Frank, *Our America*, p. 214.

Oracular.
Redolent of fermenting syrup,
Purple of the dusk,
Deep-rooted cane.

As Toomer has claimed, the Imagists 'with their insistence on fresh vision' and the 'economical line' helped to bestow upon him the tools for his 'own creation' as an artist, and *Cane*'s epigraph is an Imagist poem, conforming as it does to the avant-garde poetics of Imagism as laid down by the founders of the movement—Ezra Pound, Richard Aldington and Hilda Dolittle (H. D.)—around 1912. Imagism declared that modern poetry should insist on 'Direct treatment of the 'thing' whether subjective or objective' and use no 'superfluous' words that didn't aid in the presentation of the image itself. Eschewing what Pound would call the emotional 'gush' of nineteenth-century verse, the conventional narrative scaffolding which allowed poetry to function in similar ways to prose, and the monotony of regular rhythm and rhyme, the Imagists gave rise to the first modernist Anglo-American movement in literature. Now, Pound announced, poetry no longer told stories: it worked through the image, 'that which presents an intellectual and emotional complex in an instant of time.'[1] Toomer was well aware of the central tenets of the movement—indeed, he had written a review of an essay on Imagism by Richard Aldington in 1921[2]—and poems in free and imagistic verse would appear throughout *Cane*. But even the prose sections of Toomer's work would depend heavily upon images and motifs, rhythms and repetitions which often make *Cane*'s narrative sections function in similar ways to avant-garde poetry and the verse experiments of Robert Frost. Already, in the novel's epigraph, the reader is receiving a preview of the unique paths that *Cane* will take.

The first word of *Cane*'s epigraph, 'Oracular,' suggests that profound answers or some kind of prophecy will be found in the text that follows. The sensual images yoke disparate phenomena and ideas

---

1 Ezra Pound, *The Literary Essays of Ezra Pound*, edited by T. S. Eliot (London: Faber and Faber, 1985), pp. 3–4.
2 *Jean Toomer: Selected Essays and Literary Criticism*, pp. 3–5.

together: the fermentation of cane syrup in the refining process of sugar is an evocative scent which will permeate the southern town and cane fields presented in the first part of the book, and sweeten or sicken its descriptions accordingly. Emotive natural images like the purple of dusk will be heavy with connotations throughout, and cane itself will be identified with the deep-rooted experience of the characters in the rural landscape—the southern 'peasantry, rooted in its soil,'[1] which Toomer aspired to express in *Cane*.

3.4 The Waste Land

Alongside such rural themes, however, *Cane*'s 'oracular' opening suggests a further relationship with High modernist literature. T. S. Eliot's *The Waste Land* had recently been published by Boni and Liveright—who would also publish *Cane*—and the poem would famously use an oracular theme as its epigraph, citing on its title page the decrepit Cumaean Sibyl of ancient Greece, a prophetess who laments that she 'wants to die' because while the gods had granted her request for a long life, she had neglected to ask for eternal youth, and is now living out her endless days in misery. Arguably, the Sibylline oracle is an appropriate emblem for Eliot's difficult poem, not least because the Sybil's prophesies were written on leaves, which, should the wind scatter them or they become rearranged, 'their meaning then became incomprehensible'[2]—much as Eliot's fragmented and allusive poem has, since its appearance, encouraged and resisted interpretation in equal measure.

Arguably, we shall see that *Cane*, with its complex form, mix of genres and multiple voices, resembles no other modernist work as closely as it resembles Eliot's iconic poem. But there is a crucial difference, and this is perhaps illustrated best by William Carlos Williams' reaction to the publication of *The Waste Land*:

> … out of the blue *The Dial* brought out *The Waste Land* ... It wiped out our world as if an atom bomb had been dropped upon

---

1   *Jean Toomer: Selected Essays and Literary Criticism*, p. 11.
2   J. Lempriere, *Lempriere's Classical Dictionary* (London: Bracken Books, 1984), p. 627.

it and our brave sallies into the unknown were turned to dust.

To me especially it struck like a sardonic bullet. I felt at once that it had set me back twenty years ... Critically Eliot returned us to the classroom just at the moment when I felt that we were on the point of an escape to matters much closer to the essence of a new art form itself—rooted in the locality which should give it fruit.[1]

Like Frank, and like Toomer, Williams' poetic program sought to create a modern form of poetry rooted in an American locality; as he rightly suggests, Eliot's erudite, allusive and intertextual poem sent us back to the 'classroom'—or more specifically back to Europe, the European canon and the classics, works which *Our America* claimed had been carried from Europe by the 'principle of death.' Despite its High modernist experimentation, *Cane* remains rooted in American history and African American experience, and its intertexts send us back to the 'localities' which inspired it: cane fields, sorrow songs and ghettoes rather than an imported European canon. This social and ethnic 'rootedness' is perhaps signalled by *Cane*'s dedication, which is to his maternal grandmother—she, as Alice Walker has noted, to whom Toomer owed some of his 'dark blood.'[2]

After the epigraph and the dedication, the final detail the reader confronts before encountering the main text of *Cane* is an arc, a part of a circle which has a page to itself and prefaces the first 'southern' section of the novel. An identical but rotated arc will preface the next 'northern' section of the work, and two arcs positioned diametrically opposite each other will appear before the final section, 'Kabnis'.[3] At the end of 1922 Toomer wrote to Waldo Frank that 'CANE's design is a circle. Aesthetically, from simple forms to complex ones, and back to simple forms. Regionally, from the South up into the North, and back into the South again.'[4] The graphic arcs that introduce the

---

1   William Carlos Williams, *The Autobiography of William Carlos Williams* (New York: New Directions, 1967), p. 174.
2   Walker, *In Search of Our Mother's Gardens*, p. 65.
3   Not all editions of *Cane* faithfully reproduce these features. Rather disappointingly, Norton's most recent edition of the work (2011) doesn't even reproduce the 'Oracular' epigraph of the title page.
4   *Brother Mine: The Correspondence of Jean Toomer and Waldo Frank*, p.85.

book's three sections seem to function as symbolic parts of a 'whole' that the book's depictions of rural and urban life, and migrations from the country to the city and back, try to complete. Significantly, however, there is no completion of the circle in *Cane*: there are arcs and restless movements, just as there are stories and poems which present 'redolent' vignettes of black American experience, but, as we shall see, despite its apparent quest for answers, and the moments of beauty and revelation that it offers, in the end *Cane*, like so many works of modernist literature, will offer only incomplete and 'unfulfilled' resolutions to the questions it poses

4 Reading *Cane*

4.1 The Country and the South

Cane opens with a short prose piece titled 'Karintha,' set in the rural south. As if to conjure the atmosphere for such a setting, the story is framed by a lyric which has the form and feel of a black spiritual or 'sorrow song:'

> Her skin is like dusk on the eastern horizon,
> O cant you see it, O cant you see it,
> Her skin is like dusk on the eastern horizon
> ... When the sun goes down.[1]

'Karintha,' like a lot of Toomer's prose pieces and poems, was published separately before finally appearing between the covers of *Cane*. This opening story first appeared in the magazine *Broom* in early 1923, where it was suggested that it should be read 'accompanied by the humming of a Negro folk-song' (p. 5). One of the most unique features of *Cane* is its mix of genres and styles, but the most conspicuous example of this is its incorporation of folk forms into itself—and often at crucial points in the text. At moments of emotion and reflection, or anguish and uncertainty, what Toomer called the beautiful 'folk spirit' of the southern black communities often enters the work as a song, lyric or poetic fragment. Indeed, a few pages further along in this first section a poem will suggest that the mission of *Cane* and its author is nothing less than to preserve the voice and soul of a 'song-lit race of slaves' in the moments before they disappear:

---

1 Jean Toomer, *Cane*, second edition, edited by Rudolph P. Byrd and Henry Louis Gates Jr. (New York & London: W. W. Norton, 2011), p. 5; all subsequent references to *Cane* will be taken from this edition and given in parentheses in the body of the text. Please note that Toomer, much like James Joyce, flouted many conventions of punctuation: throughout Cane, apostrophes were omitted from contractions such as 'can't'.

... for though the sun is setting on
A song-lit race of slaves, it has not set;
Though late, O soil, it is not too late yet
To catch thy plaintive soul, leaving, soon gone,
Leaving, to catch thy plaintive soul soon gone (p. 16).

The final section of the book will present the failed poet, Ralph
Kabnis, attempting to find a language in which to express the beauty
and tragedy of the south, and throughout the work poetry and 'song'
will saturate *Cane* and exist as the work's 'privileged mode,'[1] the
expression and form which encapsulates the past and attempts to find
a future voice for the characters in the volume's pages. As we shall
see, however, in 'Karintha' the lyrical verses that frame the story
perhaps offer only an ironic contrast to the events that are narrated—
and contrasting moments of lyric beauty and disillusion will become
a defining aspect of the reader's progress through the work.

All but one of the prose pieces in the first 'southern' section of
Cane carry female names as their titles, and it is through the con-
templation of such women, and often through the narrator's desire
to possess or know them, that the urge to uncover the mystery of the
south, or discover the deep-rooted belonging that it seems to promise, takes shape. Karintha's beauty is communicated through her skin
tone, which is 'like dusk on the eastern horizon;' note that this is the
eastern not the western horizon—a vista which perhaps suggests that
her skin tone is a dusky red, like the reflected glow from a setting sun.
This oblique image is actually the start of *Cane*'s persistent refusal to
use terms like 'black' or 'white' when describing a character's skin
colour—and almost all of the characters in the volume are African
American. One of the reasons for this is, of course, Toomer's struggle against the binary and exclusivist logic of race, and his historical
insistence on 'the fact of racial intermingling.' But there is a more
sinister level of signification here too. As Charles Scruggs and Lee
Vandemarr have suggested, in the south at the time that Toomer was
writing 'Racial identity was a deadly serious matter,' and the fact of

---

1   Karen Jackson Ford, *Split-Gut Song: Jean Toomer and the Poetics of Modernity*
(Tuscaloosa: The University of Alabama Press, 2005), p. 8.

racial 'intermingling' or miscegenation is part of the 'secrecy and deadliness' that is a constant subtext of *Cane*, being 'the 'crime' that springs from the primal crime of slavery.' The sexual exploitation of black women by slave owners and others, white and black, has been a fact of American history, and even the dusky beauty of Karintha is tinged by this hidden but pervasive violence—a history of violence so pervasive that Scruggs and Vandemarr describe *Cane* as essentially a protracted 'Gothic horror story.'[1]

To be more precise, the narratives in *Cane* act like gothic detective fiction whose meanings are delivered 'in an oblique and incomplete way' and have to be reconstructed by the reader.[2] This is certainly true of 'Karintha,' a story whose setting darkens and whose subject becomes less tangible as the tale progresses. Initially, Karintha is merely a precocious child, full of vitality and energy:

> Men had always wanted her, this Karintha, even as a child, Karintha carrying beauty, perfect as dusk when the sun goes down. Old men rode her hobby-horse upon their knees. Young men danced with her at frolics when they should have been dancing with their grown-up girls. God grant us youth, secretly prayed the old men. The young fellows counted the time to pass before she would be old enough to mate with them. This interest of the male, who wishes to ripen a growing thing too soon, could mean no good to her (p. 5).

Karintha seems rather cruel and selfish, but even the preacher turns a blind eye to her deeds and 'told himself that she was as innocently lovely as a November cotton flower.' The aura of sexual threat is never far away, but when Karintha's inevitable fall occurs the narrator lays the blame at least in part upon environmental conditions and poverty:

> Homes in Georgia are most often built on the two room plan. In one, you cook and eat, in the other you sleep, and there love goes on. Karintha had seen or heard, perhaps she had felt her parents loving. One could but imitate one's parents, for to follow them

---

1 Charles Scruggs and Lee Vandemarr, *Jean Toomer and the Terrors of American History* (Philadelphia: University of Pennsylvania Press, 1998), p. 29, p. 158 and p. 111.

2 *Jean Toomer and the Terrors of American History*, p. 142.

was the way of God. She played "home" with a small boy who
was not afraid to do her bidding. (pp. 5–6).

Implicit here is the fact that Karintha's youth and beauty cannot be
safeguarded by the family; the impoverished community she lives in
seems to view her impending sexual subjugation as inevitable. All
desire her but none come forward to protect her, and soon Karintha,
forced to grow too soon, becomes a woman; but here the narrative
descends into enigmatic images and oblique lyrics:

> ... Karintha is a woman, and she has had a child. A child fell
> out of her womb onto a bed of pine-needles in the forest. Pine-
> needles are smooth and sweet. They are elastic to the feet of rab-
> bits ... A sawmill was nearby. Its pyramidal sawdust pile smoul-
> dered. It is a year before one completely burns. Meanwhile, the
> smoke curls up and hangs in odd wraiths about the trees, curls
> up, and spreads itself out over the valley ... Weeks after Karintha
> returned home the smoke was so heavy you tasted it in water.
> Some one made a song:
>
> > Smoke is on the hills, Rise up
> > Smoke is on the hills, O rise
> > And take my soul to Jesus (p. 6).

Beneath the lyrical repetition of the language—each phrase taking up
the words of the previous one in a slow accumulation of insinuation—
lies the probability that Karintha's child was born dead or killed,
and is now burning on the pyramidal sawdust pile like a sacrifice,
its soul rising to heaven through smoke as heavy and suggestive as
the fermenting cane syrup of the epigraph. As with Karintha herself,
Toomer constructs the story through a symbolism that should be
replete with images of fertility and promise but is in fact filled with
an equal sense of dangerous foreboding and death. 'Karintha' started
with a spiritual song, turned ominous with suggestions of forced
sexuality, and ends with clues that point towards an act of violence
and horror. The story ends with the reappearance of the opening
lyric; but a missed line and the repetition of the last two words lend a
menacing quality to this final refrain:

> Her skin is like dusk on the eastern horizon
> ... When the sun goes down.

> Goes down ...

In this rural setting the saw mill symbolises encroaching industrialisation, and the sinister smoke curling from its sawdust pile will drift through *Cane*'s stories and poems, reminding the reader that the countryside depicted is far from idyllic, and the apparent timelessness of the landscape is threatened by the intrusion of the modern world—as Toomer himself said of the tone of the tale, referring both to Karintha and her setting: 'the dominant emotion is a sadness derived from a sense of fading.'[1]

After the lyrical prose and disquieting conclusion of 'Karintha', the poems 'Reapers' and 'November Cotton Flower' appear to interrupt the flow of the narrative and feel rather stilted and conventional; this sense of discontinuity and contrast will, of course, become part of *Cane*'s *modus operandi*, but the sudden change in genre and mood is initially a surprise for the reader. The first poem is 8 lines long, and opens with reapers in a field, sharpening and swinging their scythes with the silence being broken only by 'the sound of steel on stones.' The final four lines thrust this vision into a more modern setting, as the reapers and scythes are replaced by horses and a mechanical mower:

> Black horses drive a mower through the weeds,
> And there, a field rat, startled, squealing bleeds,
> His belly close to ground. I see the blade,
> Blood-stained, continue cutting weeds and shade (p. 7).

There is no spacing between each set of 4 lines, but the transition and contrast is there. Toomer had lamented the coming of the mechanised victrola and player-piano to the valley of cane, and in 'Karintha' the sawmill had added to the destabilisation of the tale's pastoral setting. In 'Reapers' a similar decline is implied by the supervention of the mower, and the brutality of the final lines is emphasised by the squealing rat which the machine cuts, continuing to roll on

---

1   *Brother Mine: The Correspondence of Jean Toomer and Waldo Frank*, p. 50.

remorselessly with the vicious trochaic inversion of 'Blood-stained' disturbing the flow of the poem's iambic pentameters.

'November Cotton Flower' is slightly more complex. The title acts as a kind of warning, as it repeats a description of Karintha, whom the preacher declares to be 'as innocently lovely as a November cotton flower.' We know, however, that Karintha's physical attractiveness is part of her doom, and the slightly more irregular iambic pentameters of this sonnet tell of a coming winter:

> And cotton, scarce as any southern snow,
> Was vanishing; the branch, so pinched and slow,
> Failed in its function as the autumn rake;
> Drouth fighting soil had caused the soil to take
> All water from the streams; dead birds were found
> In wells a hundred feet below the ground—
> Such was the season when the flower bloomed.

Boll weevils, cold and drought give the first 8 lines of the sonnet (the octave) a supernatural or prophetic feel; nothing good can come of such signs. However, the sudden appearance of a cotton flower at the 'turn' into the sestet promises the restoration of normality, and even beauty. The blooming flower assumes a symbolic significance for those who see it, suggesting,

> Brown eyes that loved without a trace of fear,
> Beauty so sudden for that time of year (p. 8).

However, the 'suddenness' of the unseasonal too late or too soon flower, and the fearlessness of the loving eyes, recalls the brash vitality and early 'blooming' of Karintha—dangerous qualities in the sexually menacing environment of *Cane*'s first section. Despite the beauty which provides the sonnet's climax, it is reminiscent of Karintha's exploitation, and undercuts what might be taken as redemptive imagery with the unsettling suggestion of a false, and therefore doomed, spring.

The foreboding of 'November Cotton Flower' is borne out by the next prose section. Titled 'Becky,' it is a tale of miscegenation and death. Like Karintha, it opens and closes with a repeated fragment of text—now, however, the epigraph and coda is a stark summary rather than a spiritual lyric:

> Becky was the white woman who had two Negro sons. She's dead; they're gone away. The pines whisper to Jesus. The Bible flaps its leaves with an aimless rustle on her mound.

Portentously, in these opening lines the 'pines whisper to Jesus,' and this spiritual fragment recurs throughout the tale, but the text of the Bible remains 'aimless' and ineffective—perhaps echoing the confused 'oracular' leaves of the Sibyl in *Cane*'s opening epigraph. The narrative wastes no time in presenting the Becky as a victim of prejudice, gossip and ostracism from both sides of the community 'colour line:'

> Becky had one Negro son. Who gave it to her? Damn buck nigger, said the white folks' mouths. She wouldn't tell. Common, God-forsaken, insane white shameless wench, said the white folks' mouths. Her eyes were sunken, her neck stringy, her breasts fallen, till then. Taking their words, they filled her, like a bubble rising—then she broke. Mouth setting in a twist that held her eyes, harsh, vacant, staring ... Who gave it to her? Low-down nigger with no self-respect, said the black folks' mouths. She wouldn't tell. Poor Catholic poor-white crazy woman, said the black folks' mouths. White folks and black folks built her cabin, fed her and her growing baby, prayed secretly to God who'd put His cross upon her and cast her out (p. 9).

As a woman Becky, like Karintha, is open to sexual exploitation and subjection to the South's racial codes, but here the message is complicated by the fact that her situation negates any stereotypical ideas about white purity and seems to revel in the 'violations' of the conventions of race and gender that her behaviour displays. Eventually Becky becomes warped by the words and judgements of the town, and is portrayed as insane and shameless—haggard and accursed with sunken eyes and fallen breasts. Yet, despite the community's prayers to 'cast her out,' she and her children are fed and housed by both black and white folks. The community deny their own charitable acts, but the railroad boss allows her to live on a strip of land between the road and the railway; John Stone—a family name we will meet again at the end of this subdivision—donates the materials for her cabin, and travellers and town folk secretly leave her food and prayers. Between the modern cars on the road and the locomotives on the tracks, her one-room shack is an archaic talisman of shame—perhaps a symbol of the simultaneous modernisation and decline of the south itself. Becky seemingly oscillates in the public imaginary between being a scapegoat, a charity case, and the subject of votive offerings—a sacrificial victim, perhaps, whose plight is eased by donations prompted by collective guilt.

Becky has another son. She stays out of sight, but her mulatto sons grow up 'Sullen and cunning ... O pines, whisper to Jesus,' turn violent and eventually leave town, shouting 'godam the white folks; godam the niggers' as they leave. Nobody knows if Becky is still alive; the locals fear she is a ghost, but a 'thin wraith of smoke' (p. 10) from her chimney, reminiscent of the ominous smouldering sawdust pile in 'Karintha,' betrays her presence. The inherent pain and violence of 'racial intermingling' is starkly displayed in the tale, and the community's sympathies could actually be seen as self-serving. As Nellie McKay points out:

> Such behaviour highlights problems of communal hypocrisy and self-righteousness in a society that practices racial and sexual victimization. In her fallen state, she is important to the community, for, through her, it is able to assert its false concepts of religious and moral superiority.[1]

Becky acts as a lightning conductor for the town's indignation, but it is just as easy to read her plight, and the behaviour of the town towards her, in another way. An early re-reading of the novel suggests:

> Though Becky is condemned by men and women alike in the community, there is a spiritual bond that causes all of them, black as well as white, to honor her and to help provide her with the necessities of life. She lives in the community as a ghost, probably the ghost of a spiritual community of love.[2]

---

1   McKay, *Jean Toomer, Artist*, p. 99.
2   Benson and Dillard, *Jean Toomer*, pp. 54–5.

It could be that the denial of a human love that transcends racial boundaries is the 'hidden secret' in this gothic detective story; though Becky must suffer for her transgressions, the attempts to alleviate her hardship are tacit recognitions of her courage and the town's secret shame at their own complicity in Jim Crow injustices.

In the final paragraph of the tale, a change in narrative gear—changes which will be a regular feature of *Cane*—shifts the point of view from a summative omniscience to a local narrator, who, returning from church with his friend Barlo (another name which will return in a later prose section) witnesses the collapse of Becky's massive chimney into her hovel.

> Uncanny eclipse! Fear closed my mind. We were just about to pass ... Pines shout to Jesus! ... the ground trembled as a ghost train rumbled by. The chimney fell into the cabin. Its thud was a hollow report, ages having passed since it went off. Barlo and I were pulled out of our seats. Dragged to the door that had swung open. Through the dust we saw the bricks in a mound upon the floor. Becky, if she was there lay under them. I thought I heard a groan. Barlo, mumbling something, threw his Bible on the pile (pp. 10–11).

The final lines are shot-through with superstitious fear, and the church goers then hurry back to town to give the town crowd 'the true word' of Becky's death. Arguably, the tale's demotic descent into gothic horror merely emphasises the critique of racial segregation that is at the story's heart. The coda: 'Becky was the white woman who had two Negro sons. She's dead ... The pines whisper to Jesus. The Bible flaps its leaves with an aimless rustle ... ' underscores the tragedy and futility that 'racial intermingling' produces in a racist environment; but the tale also leaves the reader haunted by the 'community of love' that whispers, albeit ineffectively, against the savage conventions of race and desire in the south.

Next is a poem, and the first, apart from Cane's 'oracular' epigraph, which is distinctly modern in form: 'Face'.

> Hair—
> silver-gray,

> like streams of stars,
> Brows—
> recurved canoes
> quivered by the ripples blown by pain,
> Her eyes—
> mist of tears …
> condensing on the flesh below
> And her channelled muscles
> are cluster grapes of sorrow
> purple in the evening sun
> nearly ripe for worms (p.12).

If we look at the poem carefully however, and include the title in the line-count, what we have is a fractured sonnet which, like traditional love sonnets, itemises and idealises a woman's features. Here though, the imagistic telling of beauty is disturbed by the pained brow, tearful eyes and absent mouth, and the silvered hair and purple clusters of muscle suggest that we are presented with an old woman on the verge of dissolution or 'waning'—like the 'purple of the dusk' of the book's epigraph.

The ambivalence of 'Face' is echoed by a companion piece later in this section, but 'Cotton Song' is a much more traditional lyric—a work song with a religious theme:

> Come, brother, come. Lets lift it;
> Come now, hewit! roll away!
> Shackles fall upon the Judgment Day
> But lets not wait for it …
>
> Cotton bales are the fleecy way,
> Weary sinner's bare feet trod,
> Softly, softly to the throne of God,
> "We aint agwine t wait until th Judgment Day!
>
> Nassur ; nassur,
> Hump.
> Eoho, eoho, roll away!
> We aint agwine to wait until th Judgment Day!" (p.13).

Work songs connote community, communal strength and solidarity ('Come, brother ... ') and often suggest in conventional ways that the path of work leads to the throne of god and rest. After the suggested fear, violence and isolation of the previous sections, the communalism, if not the fatalism of 'Cotton Song', is a relief. However, it is well known that many work songs, spirituals, blues and other black folk forms that have the transcendence of earthly suffering as their theme, are actually coded expressions of resistance and even rebellion: the singers here 'aint agwine t wait' for Judgement day, when the stone rolls away and allows resurrection in the afterlife, for their deliverance; 'let's not wait for it' the lyric insists, in a rallying call for liberation now. 'Cotton Song' asserts community, participation and, tacitly, resistance to enslavement and the very labour it seems to celebrate. Its form is actually antiphonal, or a structure of choral call-and-response. Exemplified by the vocal exchanges between a preacher and his congregation in a black church, in music it manifests itself as a lead voice which sings a line and is then answered or echoed in the next line by another voice or chorus.[1] The call-and-response vocal form is a key feature of black American folk and religious music, and as we will see, *Cane* will return to it as a gauge of the 'spirit' of the black American south.

With 'Cotton Song' themes of resistance and hope enter the dialogic relationships between *Cane*'s juxtaposed sections.[2] However, the next section shifts the focus back to a woman in a rural community, and again sexuality causes tension and violence to erupt. 'Carma' unfolds in just three paragraphs and three lyrical interludes. The latter, identical except for the change substitution of 'corn' for 'cane' in its second appearance, introduce and conclude and thus

---

1   See Barbara E. Bowen, 'Untroubled Voice: Call and Response in *Cane*,' in Henry Louis Gates Jr (ed.), *Black Literature and Literary Theory* (London: Methuen, 1984), pp. 187–203.

2   Dialogism, or dialogic features within texts, were first theorised by Mikhail Bakhtin (1895–1975) who proposed that multiple voices and points of view interact within dialogic texts without becoming subordinated to each other or to an author's 'authoritative' viewpoint. See Raman Seldon, Peter Widdowson and Peter Brooker, *A Reader's Guide to Contemporary Literary Theory*, 5th edition (Hemel Hempstead: Harvester Wheatsheaf, 2005), pp. 40–41.

frame the story:

> Wind is in the cane. Come along.
> Cane leaves swaying, rusty with talk,
> Scratching choruses above the guinea's squawk,
> Wind is in the cane. Come along.

The rustling gossip of the cane leaves introduce Carma, who is described in the opening paragraph as a woman with a 'yellow flower face' who is 'strong as any man.' She is driving a wagon home, and the narrator follows her with his gaze, allowing her to 'feel' and return it—at the same time that his language apparently sexualises her progress through the use of innuendos common in blues and jazz lyrics: her wagon 'bumps, and groans, and shakes as it crosses the railroad tracks.' (p. 14) 'Carma', as the narrator states twice, 'is the crudest melodrama,' (p. 15) and the whole story is told in the final paragraph. Carma's husband, Bane, works away a lot; Carma takes other lovers and 'No one blames her for that,' but he picks up on the gossip when he returns one day and accuses her when he gets home. Becoming hysterical, Carma grabs a gun and runs into a canebrake. Bane hears the gun fire, and assuming she has shot herself he gathers a search party, who find her apparently lifeless and bring her home— only to discover that she was merely playing dead. Bane takes this deception as added proof of her faithlessness, senselessly attacks one of the men who found her, and ends up on the chain gang. The narrator concludes, 'Should she not take others, this Carma, strong as a man..?' (p, 15).

What the story interrogates on the surface are the sexual conventions which allow men to 'play around' but demand that women remain faithful. Carma, strong, sexual and spirited, becomes the first female in *Cane* who defies convention and emerges from the situation relatively unscathed herself. But so far only the first and third paragraphs of the tale have been discussed, and what seems crucial to the tale is the central second section, enclosed in parentheses, in which the narrator's observation of Carma returning home has prompted a reverie which allows his consciousness to move through images of the landscape, including the recurring 'web' of smoke 'spun by the spider sawdust pile' (p. 14), to a vista which permits the rural scene and a girl's singing to metamorphose into a mystical vision of Africa:

(... A girl in the yard of a whitewashed shack not much larger than the stack of worn ties piled before it, sings. Her voice is loud. Echoes, like rain, sweep the valley. Dusk takes the polish from the rails. Lights twinkle in scattered houses. From far away, a sad strong song. Pungent and composite, the smell of farm-yards is the fragrance of the woman. She does not sing; her body is a song. She is in the forest, dancing. Torches flare ... juju men, greegree, witchdoctors ... torches go out ... The Dixie Pike has grown from a goat path in Africa.

Night.

Foxie, the bitch, slicks back her ears and barks at the rising moon.) (p. 14).

This is the first time that *Cane* has made a direct link to the African heritage of its characters or narrators, and it is Carma's strength and sexual power which prompts the narrative's ecstatic plunge into the glimpse of an earthy, vital and venerated femininity which sings and dances at the heart of an African ritual. In true modernist style however, the vision is interrupted, the link with the past is broken, and the narrative returns to the Dixie Pike and a vixen barking at the Georgia moon. Carma, idealised and eroticised, becomes a link to a mythic African past and a 'rootedness' which the narrator glimpses but cannot capture or own—he is excluded by his modern self-consciousness just as Carma's 'primitive' promiscuity is ultimately disallowed by the morals of her community: to the outside world, the tale is just 'the crudest melodrama,' but to the narrator it is a revelation of a desired, if unattainable, continuity between the past and present.

'Carma's message is an ambivalent one; indeed, a contemporary review by W. E. B. du Bois had praised the ways in which *Cane* had 'dared to emancipate the colored world from the conventions of sex,' yet of 'Carma' in particular he could not see 'why Toomer could not have made the tragedy of Carma something that I could understand instead of vaguely guess at.'[1] What contemporary critics missed, despite Toomer's promptings, was that the tragedy didn't lie with Carma herself, but with the vision of lost connections and continuities that she prompts. 'Song of the Son' follows 'Carma' and suggests that the story was indeed preparing the ground for a meditation on history and heritage, for this poem has already been cited as Toomer's declaration of his attempt to preserve the voice and soul of a 'song-lit race of slaves' in their final moments. 'Song of the Son' was the first piece from what would become *Cane* to be published (it appeared in *Crisis* in April 1922) and is Toomer's most anthologised piece of work. Its iambic pentameters ask its subjects to 'Pour O pour that parting soul in song' before the decline of a race's 'sun':

> O land and soil, red soil and sweet-gum tree,
> So scant of grass, so profligate of pines,
> Now just before an epoch's sun declines
> Thy son, in time, I have returned to thee,
> Thy son, I have in time returned to thee.
>
> In time, for though the sun is setting on
> A song-lit race of slaves, it has not set;
> Though late, O soil, it is not too late yet
> To catch thy plaintive soul, leaving, soon gone,
> Leaving, to catch thy plaintive soul soon gone.
>
> O Negro slaves, dark purple ripened plums,
> Squeezed, and bursting in the pine-wood air,
> Passing, before they stripped the old tree bare
> One plum was saved for me … (p. 16).

As Karen Jackson Ford notes, this poem 'is widely recognised as *Cane*'s raison d'etre,' and its gentle rhythms 'suggest it is the lyrical heart of the book; no other moment in *Cane* so powerfully expresses the book's elegiac and commemorative mission.'[2] But even as the ancestral songs are sung and 'caught' by the artist, images which

---

1   W. E. B. du Bois and Alain Locke, 'The Younger Literary Movement' (1924), reprinted in Byrd and Gates (eds) *Cane*, pp. 184–5.

2   Ford, *Split-Gut Song*, p. 31 and p. 32.

would soon accrue rather ominous meanings disturb the surface of the poem. The first stanza features the 'sawdust glow of night' and the 'pine-smoke air' which often mingle beauty with violence in the atmosphere of *Cane*'s southern section, and the 'dark purple ripened plums' of the fourth stanza suggest the body 'nearly ripe for worms' which 'Face' had ambivalently celebrated. But the concluding stanza of 'Song of the Son' is often regarded as its most worrying, when a seed from ripened plum becomes,

> An everlasting song, a singing tree,
> Caroling softly souls of slavery,
> What they were, and what they are to me,
> Caroling softly souls of slavery.

The singing tree could easily be the tree on which slaves have been lynched for generations, and the soft carolling, caught only just in time by the poet, seems to be a lament for the murdered rather than a hymn to any kind of rebirth.

'Georgia Dusk' is similar in the ambivalence of its message. More irregular than 'Song of the Son' despite its basic five iambic beats per line, its key theme is the transformation of experience into song—but here it is the modern environment which is being hymned. Night falls 'lazily' and 'night's barbecue' begins:

> A feast of moon and men and barking hounds,
>   An orgy for some genius of the South
>   With blood-hot eyes and cane-lipped scented mouth,
> Surprised in making folk-songs from soul sounds.
>
> The sawmill blows its whistle, buzz-saws stop …
>
> Smoke from the pyramidal sawdust pile
>   Curls up, blue ghosts of trees, tarrying low
>   Where only chips and stumps are left to show
> The solid proof of former domicile.

Men and barking dogs at night often augur lynch mobs in the south, but here it is black 'cane-lipped' voices that are creating folk songs. The backdrop to this activity however is the devastated forest, reduced to stumps, chips and the sawmill's ominous smoking pile. The workers are going home, but their singing, like the singing girl in 'Carma', evokes ancestral memories of Africa:

> Meanwhile, the men, with vestiges of pomp,
>   Race memories of king and caravan,
>   High-priests, an ostrich, and a juju-man,
> Go singing through the footpaths of the swamp.

The songs rise to the stars, and the poem's final lines bestow on them the power to make mortal lips sublime, and bring dreams of Christ to the singers:

> O singers, resinous and soft your songs
>   Above the sarcred whisper of the pines,
>   Give virgin lips to cornfield concubines,
> Bring dreams of Christ to dusky cane-lipped throngs.

But what are these dreams? Don't dreams of Christ negate the 'race memories' that the songs evoked? Couldn't dreams of Christ be seen as falsehoods—consolatory tales of redemption used to subdue an exploited workforce? Even as connections with a lost history and spiritual hope are asserted, the poem's final line casts doubt over the poem's message and intensifies the uncertainties that its forerunner, 'Song of the Son', communicated.

In 'Fern' a southern woman once again functions as both an embodiment of place and a connection to the narrator's heritage. In the unexpectedly poetic opening sentence the narrator declares 'Face flowed into her eyes' (p. 18), and later, 'Like her face, the whole countryside seemed to flow into her eyes. Flowed into them with the soft listless cadence of Georgia's South.' (p. 19) Fern is of mixed race, 'Her nose was aquiline, Semitic,' and what might have been the tragedy of her conception radiates from her in the form of a religious song: 'If you have heard a Jewish cantor sing, if he has touched you and made your own sorrow seem trivial when compared with his, you will know my feeling when I follow the curves of her profile' (p. 18). Many men have known Fern but she perplexes as well as fascinates them. They make love to her but she remains apparently unsatisfied, and men stay bound to something in her which unsettles them, for 'Fern's eyes desired nothing that you could give her,' and in vain her lovers 'hungered after finding the barest trace of what she might desire.'

With 'Fern,' for the first time *Cane* presents a story delivered through the point of view of an oddly disconnected observer—one who is included in the action of the story, but who is socially as well as philosophically removed from the events he describes. In an aside the narrator reveals himself as a semi-autobiographical version of the author: '(I was from the North, and suspected of being prejudiced and stuck-up)' (p. 19), and as the tale progresses we learn only about his obsession with Fern and little, if anything, about the woman herself; like the countryside and her own desires, Fern remains mute, mysterious and unknowable. At the end of the story the narrator takes Fern for a walk at dusk, noticing that 'I felt strange, the way I always do in Georgia, particularly at dusk … It would not have surprised me had I had a vision.' He feels a mystical connection to the place, and reflects that 'When one is on the soil of one's ancestors, most anything can come to one …' (p. 21). He holds Fern, and appears to 'do' something to her that he can't remember, but she rushes away from him, hysterically cries to Jesus, sings in the darkness, and then faints in the narrator's arms.

After the narrator's fascination by the fusion of his desire for the landscape and its history that Fern's face promises, his mystical musings, his meditation on Fern's sexual history and power, and his own aborted sexual advances, it is hard not to read the story as an interrogation of motives in which the author / narrator figure undercuts his own idealising and anthropological monologues by exposing himself as ludicrous. In what might be an ironic analysis of the pitfalls of *Cane*'s project to catch the 'plaintive soul' of the south, 'Fern's narrator appears to arrogantly project his own fantasies of 'the south' onto a woman who is essentially a blank canvas. In truth, however, Fern is not a blank canvas, but an unknowable quality, and his fantasies, like his sexual advances, are confuted. The final lines of the story have the narrator regarding Fern from the window of the train which is taking him back north, and he breaks the fictional frame in order to address the reader directly:

> Saw her on her porch ... eyes vaguely focused on the sunset.
> Saw her face flow into them, the countryside and something that
> I call God, flowing into them ... And, friend, you? She is still
> living, I have reason to know. Her name, against the chance that
> you might happened down that way, is Fernie May Rosen (p.21).

Breaking the narrative frame and providing a full name to the reader
seems to be an authorial attempt to concretise Fern – to reify her and
some abstraction that he calls 'god' which she mediates. But insisting
on Fern's existence and inviting the reader to corroborate it, merely
stresses the impotence of the narrator and his inability to control or
even describe the woman and the revelations he claims she grants to
him.

This challenge to narrative authority is amplified in 'Nullo', the
following imagistic poem. The title is actually a coinage from the
Latin *nullus*, 'suggesting something invalid, insignificant, amount-
ing to nothing.'[1] The poem is comprised by what Toomer would call
the 'perfect clean economical' expression of the Imagist line, but it
seems to describe beauty that went unobserved, the inconsequence of
thought in the apprehension of natural events, and, in its final line, the
vanity of poetic imagery itself:

> A spray of pine-needles,
> Dipped in western horizon gold,
> Fell onto a path.
> Dry moulds of cow-hoofs.
> In the forest.
> Rabbits knew not of their falling,
> Nor did the forest catch aflame (p. 22).

If 'Fern' suffered from an excess of narratorial presence, 'Nullo'
dramatizes the absence of any observing consciousness or shaping
spirit. The subsequent poem, 'Evening Song' presents three stanzas
of irregularly stressed quatrains with lines of unequal length, but
whose stanzas themselves appear of identical shape typographically.
Each stanza rhymes ABBA, and the first line of each uses the moon to

---

1   Ford, *Split-Gut Song*, p. 57.

provide a conventional symbol of attachment and sympathy between two lovers.

> Cloine, curled like the sleepy waters where the moon-waves
>   start,
> Radiant, resplendently she gleams,
> Cloine dreams,
> Lips pressed against my heart (p. 23).

Unlike any other poem in *Cane*, 'Evening Song' seems to be an unqualified lovers' idyll, with no deeper or disturbing message lurking within its metaphors. It also lacks any local detail which would situate the poem in time or place, and as such is possibly the first example of a relatively naïve expression of contentment in *Cane*. It is also the last formally structured and rhymed full poem in the book—another 'swan song' perhaps—from here until the final pages of *Cane* only free verse and prose poems will feature in discrete sections. In just a few more pages the moon, too, will take on a totally different cast to what it has here.

The penultimate prose section in *Cane*'s first part is 'Esther', which gives four linked episodes from a woman's life at ages nine, sixteen, twenty two and twenty seven. Esther is a pale, mixed-race town-dwelling girl, and the bland opening of her tale brings the theme of class into play:

> Esther's hair falls in soft curls about her high cheek-boned chalk-white face. Esther's hair would be beautiful if there were more gloss to it. And if her face were not prematurely serious, one would call it pretty. Her cheeks are too flat and dead for a girl of nine. Esther looks like a little white child, starched, frilled, as she walks slowly from her home towards her father's grocery store (p. 24).

Esther's father is the richest man in the small town, and at age 22 she will be working behind the counter in his grocery store, finding herself unattractive to or rejected by black and white boys alike. At age 9 however, a large black-skinned man 'whom she has heard her father mention as King Barlo' (p. 24)—who has already thrown his Bible onto the debris in 'Becky'—falls to his knees in the street and enters a religious trance. Townsfolk gather around him, and at dusk he starts to talk. Black people 'respond' to his prophetic calls as the entranced figure outlines a myth of origins:

> ... I saw a vision. I saw a man arise an he was big an black an powerful —
>
> Some one yells, 'Preach it, preacher, preach it!'
>
> '— but his head was caught up in th clouds. An while he was agazin at th heavens, heart filled up with th Lord, some little white-ant biddies came an tied his feet to chains. They led him t th coast, they led him t th sea, they led him across th ocean an they didn't set him free. The old coast didn't miss him, an th new coast wasn't free, he left the old-coast brothers, t give birth t you an me. O Lord, great God Almighty, t give birth t you an me' (p. 25).

Barlo's parable of slave history turns into a rhymed sermon. While the sheriff swears in some deputies in case things get out of hand, Barlo's sermon gives rise to fantastic visions in Esther's young mind; later she is told of fantastic occurrences that happened that night, and, echoing a detail from the narrator's vision in 'Fern', the narrator of 'Esther' remembers the events inspiring a 'sanctified' black woman to draw 'a portrait of a black Madonna on the courthouse wall.' Esther never forgets this experience. When Barlo left town 'He left his image indelibly upon the mind of Esther. He became the starting point of the only living patterns that her mind was to know' (p. 25).

Although the narrative features Barlo, and thus links 'Esther' inter-textually to 'Becky', there are more significant links between this story and 'Carma'. In both tales the narrator has or reports a mystical vision that seems to affirm a black heritage or a black history which fills the present with meaning. Just as the narrator's desire for Carma gives him access to folk culture and memory, so the 'living patterns' of Barlo's revelation give Esther a place in the black world which her light skin and social position deny her. As years go by, Esther has a surreal sequence of prophetic dreams which feature fires, sin and black babies; she dreams of Barlo's return, and lists his 'glories' to herself. 'Black. Magnetically so. Best cotton picker in the county ... Best man with his fists, best man with dice, with a razor ... Vagrant preacher. Lover of all the women for miles and miles around. Esther decides that she loves him' (p. 26).

Esther's musings are significant here, for it is the first time that *Cane* has bestowed a psychological dimension on one of its female characters. Nellie McKay makes a convincing case that Esther is a guise for the author:

> It is significant that Esther is the only woman in the section to whom the narrator gives an interior consciousness. As his alter ego, she and her whiteness represent the gulf—in terms of education, social status, and economic advantages—that separates him from the folk culture.[1]

Barlo is to Esther what the idealised 'folk spirit' of the south is to the narrator; but if this is the case, then once again admittance, acceptance and identification are denied. Esther is 27 when the tale draws to an end. There is news of Barlo's return, and he is looking dapper and driving a new car, having 'made money on cotton during the war' (p. 27). The narrator intends warnings about Barlo's moral character to sound here, as in 1919 the author's first published essay, called 'Ghouls' and published in the *New York Call*, had been a condemnation of war profiteering.[2] Esther hears Barlo is at a bawdy house, and resolves to save him from the loose women that he is no doubt surrounded by. In a semi-trance that echoes Barlo's religious rapture of 18 years before, Esther marches into a smoky room and confronts him.

> 'Well I'm sholy damned—skuse me, but what, what brought you here, lil milk-white gal?'
> 'You.' Her voice sounds like a frightened child's that calls homeward from some point miles away.

Barlo is drunk, but he and his companions are amused when they realise what her message implies. Sniggers, hoots and hollers come from his companions, and a woman remarks 'So that's how th dictie niggers does it ... Mus give em credit fo their gall.' The middle-class

---

1 McKay, *Jean Toomer, Artist*, p. 173.
2 See Scruggs and Vandemarr, *Jean Toomer and the Terrors of American History*, pp. 52–3.

or 'dictie' Esther, whose exact intentions are as obscure to her as they are to the reader, is revolted by the drunkenly leering Barlo. She reflects that 'conception with a drunken man must be a mighty sin,' and walks out of the room like 'a somnambulist' followed by catcalls. As she exits, 'There is no air, no street, and the town has completely disappeared' (p. 28).

Esther's fate is perhaps *Cane*'s warning that the modern black American search for an 'authentic' identity is futile.[1] Whichever way we read the tale, her pilgrimage ends in failure, disillusion, and a humiliation which obliterates the world—and the final poems of *Cane*'s first section carry an equally bleak message. The short enjambed lines of 'Conversion' give a fragmented synopsis of the spiritual decline of enslaved Africans. An African 'Guardian of Souls' gets drunk and submits to the weak teachings of 'a white-faced sardonic God;' converted, the subject 'Grins, / cries / Amen, / Shouts hosanna' (p. 29). The continuity between modern black American experience and the spirit of an African heritage, so important in other sections of *Cane*; are absent in 'Conversion'—obliterated by alcohol and dogma. 'Portrait in Georgia' takes such paths of decline a step further:

> Hair—braided chestnut,
> coiled like a lyncher's rope,
> Eyes—fagots,
> Lips—old scars, or the first red blisters,
> Breach—the last sweet scent of cane,
> And her slim body, white as the ash
> of black flesh after flame (p. 30).

'Portrait in Georgia' is a companion piece to the earlier 'fractured' sonnet 'Face,' which had itemised and idealised a woman's features; here, however, any images of beauty or desire are annihilated by the imagery of lynching, violence and pain. It is impossible to tell if this is the 'portrait' of a white woman as a desired but feared object of

---

1   Edward E. Waldron suggests this in 'The Search for Identity in Jean Toomer's 'Esther," in Therman, B. O'Daniel (ed.), *Jean Toomer: A Critical Evaluation* (Washington: Howard University Press, 1988), pp. 273–6.

the gaze of a black man, or of a black or mixed-race woman whose terrible fate is being witnessed or imagined. Only the dread that the poem communicates escapes the ambivalence of this portrait, and this sets the scene perfectly for the culminating 'gothic horror' of the tale which closes *Cane*'s first southern section.

'Blood Burning Moon' is a story in three parts, and draws its title from a fragment of song which closes each of them:

> Red nigger moon. Sinner!
> Blood-burning moon. Sinner!
> Come out that fact'ry door (p. 32).

The image of the bloody moon can be found in the Bible or, as W. E. B du Bois had noted, in sorrow songs which describe the harbingers of the last judgement: 'Oh, the stars in the elements are falling, / And the moon drips away into blood.'[1] The three-line stanza with repeated first line in *Cane*'s version actually suggests a blues rather than a spiritual lyric, but whatever form it takes the opening paragraph of the story warns us that it is a bloody omen:

> Up from the skeleton stone walls, up from the rotting floor boards and the solid hand-hewn beams of oak of the pre-war cotton factory, dusk came. Up from the dusk the full moon came. Glowing like a fired pine-knot, it illumined the great door and soft showered the Negro shanties aligned along the single street of factory town. The full moon in the great door was an omen. Negro women improvised songs against its spell (p. 31).

The point of view in the story shifts between its characters, who are Louisa, a beautiful young girl who is desired by Bob Stone, the younger son of the white people she works for (and whose family had provided material for Becky's shack), and Tom Burwell, a black field hand 'whom the whole town called Big Boy' who also loves her. It is essentially the story of a love triangle and a tragedy fuelled, once again, by desire and miscegenation. Louisa is beautiful, and she sings:

Louisa sang as she came over the crest of the hill from the white

1   Du Bois, *The Souls of Black Folk*, p. 213.

folks' kitchen. Her skin was the color of oak leaves on young
trees in fall. Her breasts, firm and up-pointed like ripe acorns.
And her singing had the low murmur of winds in fig trees (p. 31).

Oblivious to the tragedy that is unfolding, Louisa thinks about Bob
Stone, whom she is soon to meet as usual in a canebrake, and she also
anticipates Tom Burwell's proposal, which she knows is imminent.
Around her dogs begin to howl, chickens cackle and roosters crow
eerily, 'heralding a weird dawn or some ungodly awakening' as she
watches the moon disappear behind cloud.

The second part of the tale opens in a clearing on the edge of the
forest where men are talking and boiling cane, drenching the area in
its sweet fragrance. Somebody unwisely mentions Louisa and some
silk stockings she probably got from Bob Stone, and Tom Burwell
knocks him down for saying it. Tom whips out a knife, but walks off
before he uses it; dogs bark, roosters crow, and Tom sees the moon
rising, prompting Cane's first clear use of interior monologue: 'He
forced his mind to fasten on Louisa. Bob Stone. Better not be' (p.
33). Tom finds Louisa on her porch and tries to tell her of his love,
but finds that 'words is like th spots on dice: no matter how y fum-
bles em, there's times when they jes wont come. I dunno why. Seems
like th love I feels fo yo done stole m tongue.' Eventually he finds
words, tells her of his love, and brags that he is nearly as good a
cotton picker as Barlo. Tom says he aims to get a farm soon with
his bosses' help, 'if ole Stone'll trust me,' so he can buy Louisa silk
stockings and dresses; and he hints at his fears about Bob Stone, to
which Louisa disingenuously replies 'I don't know what you mean,
Tom.' Tom declares that he knows she doesn't, as 'white folks aint
up t them tricks so much nowadays,' and claims portentously that if
Stone did mess with her he would 'Cut him jes like I cut a nigger'
(p.33). Ghostly shadows struggle prophetically in the rising moonlight, a woman sings and eventually Tom and Louisa and the whole
street sing of the 'Blood burning moon,' and the second part finishes.

In the final part, Bob Stone leaves his house, preparing for his
assignation with Louisa. He walks past the house which was once the
plantation cookery, and in his mind,

He saw Louisa bent over that hearth. He went in as a master should and took her. Direct, honest, bold. None of this sneaking that he had to go through now. The contrast was repulsive to him. His family had lost ground. Hell no, his family still owned the niggers, practically. Damned if they did, or he wouldnt have to duck around so. What would they think if they knew? His mother? His sister? He shouldnt mention them, shouldnt think of them in this connection (p. 34).

Looking back to his family's past standing, and feeling a mixture of love, longing and shame as a result of his desire for Louisa, his interior monologue announces his conflicted consciousness:

He was going to see Louisa to-night, and love her. She was lovely—in her way. Nigger way. What way was that? Damned if he knew. Must know. He'd known her long enough to know. Was there something about niggers that you couldnt know? Listening to them at church didnt tell you anything. Looking at them didnt tell you anything. Talking to them didnt tell you anything ... Nigger was something more. How much more? Something to be afraid of, more? Hell no. Who ever heard of being afraid of a nigger? Tom Burwell. Cartwell had told him that Tom went with Louisa after she reached home. No sir. No nigger had ever been with his girl. He'd like to see one try. Some position for him to be in. Him, Bob Stone, of the old Stone family, in a scrap with a nigger over a nigger girl. In the good old days ... Ha! Those were the days. His family had lost ground. Not so much, though ... She was worth it. Beautiful nigger gal. Why nigger? Why not, just gal? No, it was because she was nigger that he went to her. Sweet ... The scent of boiling cane came to him (pp. 34–5).

Following the smell of cane Bob Stone overhears men talking about Tom and Louisa; enraged, he runs to her house and confronts them. A fight ensues, Bob Stone's is beaten by Tom, Stone draws a knife and Tom draws his own. In the bloody drama that ensues, Bob Stone's throat is cut, and he staggers into town and gasps Tom's name. Tom just stands rooted to the spot outside Louisa's house, while the lynch mob arrive, drag him into the old factory and burn him at the stake:

'Stench of burning flesh soaked the air' (p. 37).

The themes of violence and miscegenation which have run through *Cane*'s sketches and poems are focused in this story, and the 'primal crime' of slavery is treated directly. Here, the history of sexual abuse—which degraded black men at the same time as it brutalised black women—as it was practiced by white slave owners is revealed. The lynch law of the south supposedly existed to ensure the virtue of white women against the lusts of black men, but 'Blood Burning Moon' presents us with the much more historically accurate situation of the white man assuming sexual rights over his workers: 'Bob Stone, of the old Stone family, in a scrap with a nigger over a nigger girl. In the good old days ... Ha!' But the old days have gone. The tale begins and ends in a ruined factory, a pre-war cotton factory with 'skeleton stone walls' and 'rotting floor boards' which imply that the economic power of the south is waning, just as the social power of the slave owner has, or should have disappeared. Like a gothic horror that haunts the present, however, the past returns to perpetrate its violence. Tom Burwell is dragged to the ruined factory and murdered; his face is 'set and stony,' and his head is erect until it eventually falls forward in the flames. The black man keeps his dignity, but little else. For Louisa, there is only the madness of grief, and song:

> The full moon, an evil thing, an omen, soft showering the homes of folks she knew. Where were they, these people? She'd sing, and perhaps they'd come out and join her. Perhaps Tom Burwell would come. At any rate, the full moon in the great door was an omen which she must sing to ... (p. 37).

Louisa sings, but who will come out to join her on such a night? She calls, but at the end of *Cane*'s first southern section, there is no response.

4.2 The City and the North

The contrast between the first and second sections of *Cane* could hardly be greater, and it intensifies the northern / southern, rural / urban divide. 'Seventh Street' opens and closes with a lyric; it isn't a 'sorrow song', but something like a jazz rap celebrating the fast, loose and flashy lives of urban liquor bootleggers.

> Money burns the pocket, pocket hurts,
> Bootleggers in silken shirts,
> Ballooned, zooming Cadillacs,
> Whizzing, whizzing down the street-car tracks (p. 41).

The Washington D. C. scene with its money, silk shirts and fast cars provides a disorientating transition from the factory town lynching that the reader has just witnessed, but this just emphasises the fact that we are now in another place and almost another time. We are also meeting a new ingredient in *Cane*'s generic mix for the first time—not lyrical prose: that belongs to the south and its 'songs,' but the fierce, disjunctive and unexpected imagery of the modernist prose poem:

> Seventh Street is a bastard of Prohibition and the War. A crude-boned, soft-skinned wedge of nigger life breathing its loafer air, jazz songs and love, thrusting unconscious rhythms, black reddish blood into the white and whitewashed wood of Washington. Stale soggy wood of Washington. Wedges rust in soggy wood ... Split it! In two! Again! Shred it! ... the sun. Wedges are brilliant in the sun; ribbons of wet wood dry and blow away. Black reddish blood. Pouring for crude-boned soft-skinned life, who set you flowing? (p,41).

Seventh Street is a 'bastard' because it is a district populated by recent migrants from the south: families, unskilled workers and demobbed soldiers looking for new opportunities in the northern city, leaving behind the Jim Crow horrors of the south, and taking advantage of an underground bootleg economy.[1] These are the things which set this new black blood 'flowing' into and around Seventh Street. The imagery of the poem suggests this new black proletarian population, its energy and its popular culture—'its loafer air, jazz songs and love'—is forcing a wedge of new blood, sun and vigour into the stale 'whitewash' of Washington. It is not only the white population which

---

1   Kerman and Eldridge, *The Lives of Jean Toomer*, p. 84.

is signified by these images of white soggy wood, but also the complacent black bourgeois residents of the city—and Toomer himself is a member of just such an elite.

Stressing its difference from *Cane*'s first subdivision, 'Seventh Street' seemingly disavows the bucolic archetypes of the south for a futuristic hymn to the city and technology. In 1923, in the literary magazine *S4N*, Toomer had written of art's 'necessary' acceptance of the machine and the metaphors of power that it grants to modern life and art—'The life around me is pregnant and warm, dynamic, tensioned, massed, jazzed, lovable … I want great art … I want great substance, great power.'[1] Using the energy of new black blood to further dismantle the apparatus of the south and the past 'Seventh Street' claims that even god couldn't stomach the blood flowing here, and sets up a 'Nigger God!' in his place. The city seems to offer energy and futuristic promise. But attention to the context soon tells us that the north, too, is a racial tinderbox—as the wave of riots which swept America in the 'red summer' of 1919 proved. Seventh Street was actually the hub of four days of Washington race riots in July of that year, when whites, many of them soldiers, had attacked black people and residential areas after rumours that a white woman had been raped; the black population fought back after the police failed to intervene, a wave of new and energetic resistance that Toomer endorsed in his essay 'Reflections on the Race Riots' which appeared in the *Call* in August of that year.[2] The differences between the north and the south are perhaps not so profound, after all.

The next section is a *kind* of prose poem, but it is also one of the most surreal pieces to appear in *Cane*—or indeed any other modernist work. Titled 'Rhobert', it is a portrait of a man under pressure:

> Rhobert wears a house, like a monstrous diver's helmet, on his head. His legs are banty-bowed and shaky because as a child he had rickets. He is way down. Rods of the house like antennae of a dead thing, stuffed, prop up in the air. He is way down. He is sinking. His house is a dead thing that weighs him down.

---

1   *Jean Toomer: Selected Essays and Literary Criticism*, pp. 19–20.
2   See Scruggs and Vandemarr, *Jean Toomer and the Terrors of American History*, p. 54.

> He is sinking as a diver would sink in mud should the water
> be drawn off. Life is a murky, wiggling, microscopic water that
> compresses him. Compresses his helmet and would crush it the
> minute that he pulled his head out. He has to keep it in (p. 42).

Compressed and oppressed, Rhobert could be a personification of
the black urban middle class—free of the terrors of the south but
now overloaded with material possessions and anxieties about them.
However, the section's imagery follows a logic which resists any
straightforward interpretation. Diseased and surrounded by mud,
water and 'microscopic' life, allowing his monstrous helmet to
convince him of the safety and 'practical infinity' of the space inside
it and caring 'not too straws as to whether or not he will ever see his
wife and children again.' Rhobert has been dehumanised by this alien
environment; that however is all that the reader can be sure of—that
the story symbolically presents an inhuman and alien environment.

Clues to the meaning of the section abound, but none really satisfy all of its embryonic narrative elements. Rhobert is an anagram
of 'brother,' and as such suggests kinship and sympathy with the
character portrayed. The only clear statement about the origin of the
house is that 'God built the house. He blew His breath into its stuff-
ing. It is good to die obeying Him who can do these things.' If the
house is merely a metaphor for the church, however, then surely the
power of the church is more potent in the rural south than the mod-
ernised north? The final lines of the section see Rhobert sinking, and
the narrator implores us to sing for him:

> ... open our throats, brother, and sing "Deep River" when he
> goes down.

> Brother, Rhobert is sinking.
> Lets open our throats, brother,
> Lets sing Deep River when he goes down (p. 43).

'Deep River' is one of the best known spirituals, but its message—
'my home is over Jordan;' 'I want to cross over into camp ground'—
is ambiguous; the freedom of death is what is on the other side of the
deep river, and this sheds a rather gory light on 'Rhobert's plea to

'open' our throats. What is clear at this point in *Cane* is that song is no longer the privileged medium which carries the spirit of the folk culture; it has become something desired but ineffectual, something significant but lost. The folk spirit appears in this section of *Cane* as a source of replenishment that can't be reached—something from the past which has become mythic: thus 'Deep River' perhaps functions in the alienated environment of 'Rhobert' like allusions to Ovid function in Eliot's *The Waste Land*.

After the brash urbanism and the opaque surrealism of the first two pieces in *Cane*'s second subdivision, the next prose piece, 'Avey,' is a realist narrative that feels like an echo, in title, style and theme, of the southern sections of the book. Indeed, 'Avey' is an 'urban' companion piece to 'Fern,' for again the narrator is a semi-autobiographical version of the author, and the eponymous woman is, like Fern (and most other female characters in *Cane*), a mysterious, alluring and elusive character that the narrator yearns to understand.

The story is in five sections, and opens with the narrator at the age of sexual awakening. He hangs around with his friends in the street, sitting on the curb alongside 'young trees which had not outgrown their boxes,' which the boys used to whittle with their knives; the narrator feels an affinity with the trees that seemed to whinny 'like colts impatient to be let free.' They watch Avey leave a man's apartment, aloof and indifferent to the presence of the boys who 'talked dirt,' and speculated about her lover and love life—one of them, Ned, in his new long pants, bragging 'Hell, I bet I could get her too if you little niggers weren't always spying and crabbing everything' (p. 44). At the outset the narrator had declared that he 'came to love her, timidly,' and as time passes he continues to try to impress her, but even when they are together on a riverboat and she takes him in her arms, the narrator 'could feel by the touch of it that it wasn't man-to-woman love' (p. 45). He kisses her, trying to 'break through her tenderness to passion,' but she just hums a lullaby. The narrator talks because he 'knew damned well that I could beat her at that,' but she remains so wistful and inattentive that eventually the narrator gives up to 'let her love me, silently, in her own way' (pp. 45–6). The next section takes place 'the following summer at Harpers Ferry'—the location of the failed slave revolt of 1859 which was a catalyst for the Civil War, and a 'black' resort where Toomer spent many summers. Avey still manages to cool the narrator's ardour, but he seems to have made love to her despite her passivity. They stay together at a boarding house and he worries about the scandal, as gossip might stop her getting employment as a teacher, but 'She didn't care.' Eventually, the narrator begins to resent her apparent indifference: 'As time went on, her indifference to things began to pique me ... yes, hell, that's what it was, her downright laziness. Sloppy indolence' (p. 46). He goes away to college and hears only bad reports of her—his old friend Ned saying 'She was no better than a whore' (p.47).

Whether Avey is a prostitute or not isn't made clear in the story; but she is a woman, like Carma in *Cane*'s southern subdivision, who isn't limited by the conventions of her environment. Five years pass, but the narrator is still fascinated by her. Hearing she is in New York he travels there and gets a job, but doesn't find her. Returning to Washington he meets her by chance on an evening suffused by an image drawn from 'Karintha's lyric epigraph: 'One evening in early June, just at the time when dusk is most lovely on the eastern horizon, I saw Avey, indolent as ever, leaning on the arm of a man.' He asks if she will walk with him and he takes her to a park on high ground, where the mood changes as the narrator reflects that: 'Washington lies below ... And when the wind is from the South, soil of my homeland falls like a fertile shower upon the lean streets of the city.' The reader knows by now that the 'homeland' referred to is a spiritual, rather than an actual home, and that the desire for the fertile influence of the south is a romantic wish on the part of the narrator, one that is inextricably linked with his longing for Avey. They can hear a band playing in the distance, but the narrator 'wanted the Howard Glee club to sing 'Deep River,' from the road. To sing 'Deep River, Deep River,' from the road ... ' (p. 48). and the narrator begins to hum a folk tune. This is the first time that the lyrical spirit of the south has fully entered the second section of *Cane*, but there is a distancing irony in the fact that the narrator imagines 'Deep River' sung by a university choir, and not a folk song emerging from the 'valley of cane.' The couple sit, and the narrator counsels Avey about her life, and speaks about his own hopes as an artist:

> I pointed out that in lieu of proper channels, her emotions had
> overflowed into paths that dissipated them. I talked, beautifully I
> thought, about an art that would be born, an art that would open
> the way for women the likes of her. I asked her to hope, and build
> up an inner life against the coming of that day. I recited some of
> my own things to her. I sang, with a strange quiver in my voice,
> a promise-song. And then I began to wonder why her hand had
> not once returned a single pressure.

Avey has fallen asleep, and the narrator sits beside her through the
night, watching dawn break over the capitol. Here, as in 'Fern,' the
narrator's attempts to know, control or manipulate a desired woman
sexually, or valorise her as a portal to cultural identity or connection,
are frustrated, and he ends sleepless, cerebral and ludicrous, as she
slumbers. Despite her calm, in a sense it is Avey rather than the
narrator who is out of place in the city; she is an echo of the south,
something past, and her nonchalant promiscuity and quiet tenderness
fascinate the narrator as vestiges of a desired folk spirit. As *Cane*
has shown us however, this departing spirit is something that eludes
lover and artist alike, and the struggle to discover 'an art that would
open the way' remains an empty ideal—but one which will resurface
dramatically in the book's final dramatic subdivision.

The first formal poems of *Cane*'s second section follow 'Avey.'
'Beehive' is a fourteen-line poem in free verse—another 'fractured
sonnet'—which uses the hive as a metaphor for the black city:

> Within this black hive to-night
> There swarm a million bees;
> Bees passing in and out the moon ...
> Silver honey dripping from the swarm of bees (p. 50).

The honey is a valuable product of the hive's labours: perhaps it is
culture, or love, or community and the riches contained in social
relationships. The poet appears, and presents himself as a 'drone,'
one who does no work but gets drunk on the hive's produce:

> And I, a drone,

> Lying on my back,
> Lipping honey,
> Getting drunk with silver honey,
> Wish that I might fly out past the moon
> And curl forever in some far-off farmyard flower.

Like the narrator of 'Avey,' the artist here is located in the city, but his dreams are filled with the south, a place where he can 'curl forever in some far-off farmyard flower.' The image of dripping honey recurs in the second poem, 'Storm Ending,' where 'Thunder blossoms' like 'Great, hollow, bell-like flowers,' but the 'Full-lipped flowers' that drip the rain 'like honey' are 'Bitten by the sun,' suggesting that here we have black women ('flowers') from the south who are either receiving the storm's nourishing rain or, reversing the nurturing metaphor, it is causing them to 'bleed:'

> Full-lipped flowers
> Bitten by the sun
> Bleeding rain
> Dripping rain like golden honey—
> And the sweet earth flying from the thunder (p.50).

The final line of this imagist text does little to help the reader to dispel the ambivalence of the message, and 'Storm Ending's imagery, despite being rooted in nature, is shot through with connotations of violence, suffering and flight.

'Theater' plunges back into the heart of Washington's black urban culture, and, along with 'Box Seat,' is the first of two prose pieces inspired by Toomer's two-week appointment as assistant manager at the Howard Theater in September 1922.[1] 'Theater' is set in the Howard Theater near Seventh Street (the more up-market Lincoln Theater features in 'Box Seat') and its opening lines are reminiscent of the brash prose poetry of 'Seventh Street'—but here the prose performs a paean to the anarchic energy of black popular culture:

Life of nigger alleys, of pool rooms and restaurants and near-

---

1   See *Brother Mine: The Correspondence of Jean Toomer and Waldo Frank*, p.64 and p. 68.

> beer saloons soaks into the walls of Howard Theater and sets
> them throbbing jazz songs. Black skinned, they dance and shout
> above the tick and trill of white-walled buildings. At night, they
> open doors to people who come in to stamp their feet and shout.
> At night, road shows volley songs into the mass-heart of black
> people. Songs soak the walls and seep out to the nigger life of
> alleys and near-beer saloons, of the Poodle Dog and Black Bear
> cabarets. Afternoons, the house is dark, and the walls are sleep-
> ing singers until rehearsal begins. Or until John comes within
> them (p. 51).

Like the black blood that 'Seventh Street' had seen driven into
Washington's whitewashed wood, here jazz music soaks into walls,
makes them throb with life and turns the architectural fabric of the
city into the cultural antithesis of Rhobert's imprisoning bourgeois
house. However, complicated class issues are raised immediately with
the introduction of John, 'the manager's brother,' who is watching
rehearsals. The text informs us that 'Light streaks down upon him
from a window high above. One half his face is orange in it. One half
his face is in shadow … John's mind coincides with the shaft of light.'
The significance of this image soon becomes clear, as in 'Theater'
interior monologue is used extensively to expose the psychology of
the characters. John watches the female dancers assemble and 'tries
to trace origins and plot destinies;' as the director spurs the girls on to
energise and eroticise their movements '(Lift your skirts, Baby, and
talk t papa!),' John muses:

> John: Soon the director will herd you, my full-lipped, distant
> beauties, and tame you, and blunt your sharp thrusts in loosely
> suggestive movements, appropriate to Broadway. (O dance!)
> Soon the audience will paint your dusk faces white, and call you
> beautiful. (O dance!) Soon I … (O dance!) I'd like … (pp. 51–2).

John is affected by the sexual energy on display '(O dance!)' but
reflects that soon they will be tamed and made to fit into a respectable
Broadway mould for the audience, their thrusts blunted and their
dusk faces whitened. John, like so many of the male characters and
narrators in *Cane*, is lamenting the way in which the 'primitivism'

of the dancers will be stifled by modern morals and expectations, and he spots one in particular, Dorris, who, with her black hair, purple stockings and 'lemon-colored face,' prompts erotic thoughts. However, John desires her, but 'Holds off:'

> John: Stage-door johnny; chorus-girl. No, that would be all right. Dictie, educated, stuck-up; show girl. Yep. Her suspicion would be stronger than her passion. It wouldn't work. Keep her loveli-ness. Let her go (p.52).

John's disjunctive train of thought is hard to follow here, but the text soon tells us that the judgements 'Dictie, educated, stuck-up' are what he imagines Dorris the show girl would apply to him; as one of dancers tells Dorris when she asks about John: 'Dictie: Nothin doin, hon.' The earlier chiaroscuro lighting that 'John's mind coincides with' symbolises a split between his desire for what he considers to be the dark, primitive and instinctive aspect of the scene in front of him, and his own 'educated' bourgeois reserve and timidity. 'Theater's internal monologues display the complex friction between sexual desire and social convention, and as Dorris tries to seduce him with her dance, she becomes the first woman that *Cane* grants full psychological access to:

> Dorris: I bet he can love. Hell, he cant love. He's too skinny. His lips are too skinny. He wouldn't love me anyway, only for that. But I'd get a pair of silk stockings out of it. Red silk. I got purple. Cut it, kid. You cant win him to respect you that away. He wouldnt anyway. Maybe he would. Maybe he'd love. I've heard em say that men who look like him (what does he look like?) will marry if they love. O will you love me? And give me kids, and a home, and everything? (I'd like to make your nest, and honest, hon, I wouldn't run out on you.) You will if I make you. Just watch me (p. 53).

Dorris dances, and the narrator imagines that her muscles and limbs are producing 'Glorious songs … And her singing is of canebrake loves and mangrove feastings' (p. 54). The text makes a link between Dorris and the desire for the spirit of the south, but it is reinforced a few lines later in a curious passage that is indented, in a smaller type face, and is introduced as 'John dreams.' The narrative here is transformed into a third-person stage-direction which describes John imagining a meeting between Dorris and himself in a back alley; despite the urban setting there are autumn leaves on the ground, and Dorris wears a perfume 'Of old flowers, or of a southern canefield.' Dorris carries with her the atmosphere of a past, mythic time, but at the end of the dream the educated John 'reaches for a manuscript of his, and reads,' and when Dorris finishes dancing she looks to him only to find that his face 'is a dead thing in the shadow which is his dream;' finally, she runs to her dressing room and weeps with disappointment as her friend reminds her 'I told you nothing doin.'

Cane's treatment of the tensions between self-conscious narrators, the allure of the folk spirit, sensual beauty, the stunting effects of social convention and the desire for instinctive passion, come to a head in 'Theater', but there is no resolution of the conflict between them. Indeed, it seems that even the energies of black popular culture merely highlight deeper losses that *Cane* laments. The dancing is described as 'monotonous' and doomed for Broadway mediocrity; the jazz is 'discordant' (p. 51), and even though Dorris' dancing transforms itself into 'Glorious songs' they don't bridge the gap between Dorris and John, or the dictie observer and his dreams of 'canebrake loves.' As Karen Jackson Ford notes, in 'Theater' the energy of dance cannot make up for the loss of the folk song, and the second part of *Cane*,

> … repeatedly demonstrates that what appears to be revivifying energy and activity may actually be frenzied desperation. As the culture of the city music hall gains power, the culture of the slaves, and their African ancestors and southern descendants, fades.[1]

The two texts that follow 'Theatre' are, along with 'Rhobert,' the most surreal episodes between *Cane*'s covers. 'Her Lips Are Copper Wire' appears to be a love poem that expresses itself through an urban and technological Imagist vocabulary:

---

1   Ford, *Split-Gut Song*, p. 99.

whisper of yellow globes
gleaming on lamp-posts that sway
like bootleg licker drinkers in the fog

and let your breath be moist against me
like bright beads on yellow globes

telephone the power-house
that the main wires are insulate

(her words play softly up and down
dewy corridors of billboards)

then with your tongue remove the tape
and press your lips to mine
till they are incandescent (p. 55).

There is no punctuation and the stanzas show only the barest development of any narrative elements, and although the one study that concentrates on Toomer's poetry calls this 'the most misread poem in *Cane*'[1] it is hard to know how to read its ambiguous images aright. The radical modernist form and technological focus suggest that here we have a celebration of the city or an attempt to splice together contemporary urban themes and a romantic encounter. However, the title itself raises a question mark over this approach. Throughout *Cane*, beauty has been 'full-lipped;' copper lips would conduct the electricity of a kiss well, but copper *wire* seems to undercut the erotic charge at the outset here. Comparing a lover's breath to condensation on street lights is, again, disconcerting, and some main wires may be 'insulate,' but removing tape from electrical circuitry suggests an incandescent shock rather than a kiss. What the poem might present is a symptomatic *failure* of the language of love divorced from the tradition of lyric and song.

Failure because of alienation from a vital source is also be a theme of the next text, the three-paragraph prose poem 'Calling Jesus', whose first and last paragraphs open with the same phrase: 'Her soul is like a little thrust-tailed dog that follows her, whimpering' (p. 56). As

---

1 Ford, *Split-Gut Song*, p.80.

with 'Rhobert,' the urban house is a site and symbol of constraint and repression, for each night the woman comes home and her dog-soul is shut out by the storm door, 'left in the vestibule, filled with chills till morning.' At night, somebody steals in and carries it to where she sleeps, 'upon clean hay cut in her dreams' or 'cradled in dream-fluted cane.' The dog-soul is actually the memory of the south which can't enter the respectable house, but, with the field holler 'eoho' which featured in 'Cotton Song,' and the comfort of 'the milk-pod cheek of Christ,' memories of the south can walk into dreams 'soft as the bare feet of Christ moving across bales of southern cotton.'

The surreal tone of 'Calling Jesus' is playful, but urban alienation and the consolation of dreams of a mythic south take a more psychotic turn in the story 'Box Seat.' Split into two parts, the first section sees Dan Moore, a 'poor man out of work,' calling on his sweetheart Muriel, a teacher who rooms with Mrs Pribby, a respectable white woman. The opening lines exploit fully *Cane*'s opposition between white urban repression and the crude vigour of the black life that 'sings' seductively in its streets:

> Houses are shy girls whose eyes shine reticently upon the dusky body of the street. Upon the gleaming limbs and asphalt torso of a dreaming nigger. Shake your curled wool-blossoms nigger. Open your liver lips to the lean, white spring. Stir the root-life of a withered people. Call them from their houses, and teach them to dream.
>
> Dark swaying forms of Negros are street songs that woo virginal houses (p. 57).

The 'Box Seat' of the title becomes a metaphor for being 'boxed in' which the story returns to constantly. But the figure of Dan doesn't 'woo' the urban houses so much as angrily storm them. On finding Muriel's house Dan can't find the bell; fumbling, and worrying that he might be mistaken for a burglar, his interior monologue follows dark courses, and something of the gothic horror that featured in Cane's southern subdivision rears its head:

> Dan: Break in. Get an ax and smash in. Smash in their faces. I'll show em ... I'll show em. Grab an ax and brain em. Cut em up.

Jack the Ripper. Baboon from the zoo. And then the Cops come. 'No, I aint a baboon. I aint Jack the Ripper. I'm a poor man out of work. Take your hands off me, you bull-necked bears. Look into my eyes. I am Dan Moore. I was born in a canefield. The hands of Jesus touched me. I am come to a sick world to heal it.'

Dan's violent thoughts anticipate others' judgements, but these segue into claims of a southern birth that he sees as blessed, which then turns prophetic and disturbingly delusional.

Prophetic visions of a mythic black messiah will recur in the story, but the middle-class home where Muriel boards is equally disturbing in its repressive respectability. After Mrs Pribby lets Dan into the house, he waits for Muriel while Mrs Pribby sits down to read a news-paper and keep an eye on Dan, to ensure that nothing untoward passes between him and her lodger. As she sits, 'There is a sharp click as she fits into her chair and draws it to the table.' It sounds like a bolt being shot into place, and violent thoughts erupt inside Dan as he feels that the house 'contracts around him,' and Mrs Pribby's house bolts itself to all the other houses 'which belong to Mrs Pribbys' (p.58). Reacting to the nightmare of steel boxes—reminiscent of 'Rhobert'—which the houses have become in his mind, Dan puts his ear against the wall and hears a rumble 'that comes from the earth's deep core,' the sound of 'powerful underground races' which augur 'The next world-sav-iour coming up that way … The new-world Christ ….' His descent into messianic visions is halted by the arrival of Muriel, who is rather put out by his presence. Muriel 'clicks' into a chair, but Dan becomes earnest and passionate, mysteriously mentioning something about the pain of 'the last few months.' Whatever caused this pain, Muriel wishes to avoid the subject, and she draws back, repeatedly warning him that Mrs Pribby will overhear them, and her interior monologue exposes her fear of the scandal that Dan's impulsiveness threatens to cause and her own entrapment in the straitjacket of social expectation and respectability: 'Muriel: Shame about Dan. Something awfully good and fine about him. But he don't fit in.' She has tried to love Dan, but she thinks of Mrs Pribby and asks: 'What has she got to do with me? She *is* me, somehow. No she's not. Yes she is. She is the town, and the town won't let me love you, Dan' (p. 59). The narrator pushes the metaphorical struggle between instinctive emotions and respectable repression further, stating that Dan persists in his struggle with Muriel because 'Her animalism, still unconquered by zoo-restrictions and keeper-taboos, stirs him.' He responds savagely to Muriel's claim that all she wants is to make people happy by insisting that her 'aim is wrong:'

> There is no such thing as happiness. Life bends joy and pain, beauty and ugliness, in such a way that no one may isolate them. No one should want to. Perfect joy, or perfect pain, with no contrasting element to define them, would mean a monotony of consciousness, would mean death. Not happy, Muriel. Say that you have tried to make them create (p. 60).

This insistence on friction, on a painful dialectic between joy and pain, is something that Toomer had insisted upon in 'The South in Literature,' which stressed the 'pain and joy ... ugliness and beauty' of his themes, and it is a friction that the final section of *Cane* will suggest it is the task of the artist to confront. But in 'Box Seat' it merely exacerbates the conflict between the couple. Muriel has informed Dan that she is going to the theatre with a friend later, Dan advances on her, she retreats, Mrs Pribby starts to rise indignantly, and Dan leaves, slamming the door.

The second part of the story opens in the Lincoln Theater, a 'superior' establishment to the Howard—where John watched Dorris dance—as it didn't feature popular jazz and blues artists, but catered for more respectable tastes with a variety bill for a middle-class audience.[1] However, even in this genteel establishment the kind of primal. messianic and paranoid impulses that Dan represents keep disturbing the flow of the narrative:

> People come in slowly ... "— for my Sunday go-to-meeting dress, O glory God! O shout Amen!" ... and fill the vacant seats of Lincoln Theater. Each one is a bolt that shoots into a slot, and is locked there (p. 62).

---

1   See Scruggs and Vandemarr, *Jean Toomer and the Terrors of American History*, p. 164 and p. 176.

The exclamations to god recall the primitive 'shouting' which the town population had objected to in the valley of cane's folk songs, and here in the theatre Muriel, already in her box seat, tries to ignore Dan as she sees him ushered down the aisle, and her fears about his passion take an extreme form in her thoughts: 'He mustn't see me ... He can't reach me ... He'd put his head down like a goring bull and charge me. He'd trample them. He'd gore. He'd rape!' In getting to his seat Dan treads on a man's corns, then sits beside a 'portly Negress' who he imagines to be an earthy symbol of ancestral connections: 'A soil-soaked fragrance comes from her ... Her strong roots sink down and disappear in blood-lines that waver south' (p. 63). A vision of 'a new world Christ' accompanies his dreaming, but when he shakes himself free of its spell he finds that the woman's eyes 'look at him unpleasantly' and, as happens with many of the male characters who use women as portals to the folk spirits of the south, his vision collapses. The performance starts and Dan mutters, fidgets and upsets his neighbours—almost coming to blows with the man whose feet he had trodden on. On stage, an equally brutal and bizarre act involving two dwarves dressed as prize fighters who 'pound and bruise and bleed each other' (p. 64) is taking place. Dan's musings take him into a strange theoretical refutation of feminism by way of a mechanistic / imagistic model of sexual intercourse—'Me, horizontally above her. / Action: perfect strokes downward oblique'—which descends into pompous statements about the 'machine-age design' of such an activity, while, grotesquely, in the objective world of the theatre, the dwarves 'pound each other furiously' (p. 65), the audience wants more, but they are led bleeding from the stage. While the audience applauds the text plunges us into another of Dan's reveries; spotting an old man he muses about the man's past, thinking that he was born in slavery—'Slavery not so long ago. He'll die in his chair. Swing low, sweet chariot.' Wondering if the old man knew Walt Whitman or saw the leaders of the Civil War, Dan's thoughts become incoherent, and he appears to ask the old man about the 'rumbling underground' that he had heard earlier, while on stage one of the dwarves sings and holds a mirror so that light is shone onto the various audience members that he directs his song to, and he offers Muriel a blood spattered rose.

The story comes to a climax when Dan, his head filled with absurd visions of god-like power and retribution, imagines flashing lightning—only to find that the apocalyptic lightning is the mirror being trained on him by the dwarf, dispelling the grandeur of his imagined acts with the ludicrous proceedings unfolding on the stage. The dwarf has offered Muriel the bloody rose, but she flinches from it and from him; this prompts several narrative lines to intersect and cross in what looks like a fragmented imagist poem. The dwarf silently pleads with Muriel to overcome her revulsion, overlook his deformity and accept the rose, as he, too, is a divine creation; at the same time the alternating italicised lines represent Dan's thoughts, who seems to see 'the wisdom and tenderness,' 'suffering and beauty' of the actor:

> Words form in the eyes of the dwarf:
>
> Do not shrink. Do not be afraid of me.
> *Jesus*
> See how my eyes look at you.
> *the Son of God*
> I too was made in His image.
> *was once—*
> I give you the rose.
>
> Muriel, tight in her revulsion, sees black, and daintily reaches for the offering. As her hand touches it, Dan springs up from his seat and shouts:
> "JESUS WAS ONCE A LEPER!" (p.67).

Dan's outburst seems almost logical to the reader, given our access to his disturbing prophetic visions, but to his neighbours he just seems crazy. Trying to leave, he steps on the same man's corns again, they argue, and go out into the alley to fight; 'Eyes of houses, soft girl-eyes' look upon the crowd; the man takes off his coat for a fight but Dan, 'having forgotten him, keeps going.'

The inconsequential ending of 'Box Seat' emphasises the unsatisfactory alternatives that the story offers to the reader. Dan is a misfit in the city; he dreams of the south and some kind of messianic deliverance, but whereas until now the south has featured as a myth in this subdivision of *Cane*, a heritage that is still beautiful and significant even as it moves out of reach, for Dan this loss has sent him over an edge: Dan is a study in disillusion leading to psychosis, a character traumatised by his historical situation and environment in a way that, under two years later, the shell-shock victim Septimus Smith would be in Virginia Woolf's modernist classic *Mrs Dalloway* (1925). But Muriel, too, is just as damaged. Repressed, 'boxed in' to a respectability that won't even allow her to talk about recent pain (significantly, the reader never learns the nature of this pain as the narrative represses it just as Muriel does) and terrified of the scandal any emotional display might cause, she seems, like the woman in 'Calling Jesus', to have left her soul outside in the cold city streets.

Unsurprisingly, *Cane*'s final poems offer little resolution or comfort. 'Prayer' is another fourteen-line fractured sonnet, and like 'Portrait in Georgia' and 'Face', it presents fragments of a body and a self. But here the parts are different—they are the soul, body and mind:

> My body is opaque to the soul ...
> But my mind, too, is opaque to the soul.
> A closed lid is my soul's flesh-eye ...
> (How strong a thing is the little finger!)
> So weak that I have confused the body with the soul,
> And the body with its little finger.
> (How frail is the little finger.)
> My voice could not carry to you did you dwell in stars,
> O Spirits of whom my soul is but a little finger ... (p. 68).

What the poem leaves us with is a sense of the blindness of this trinity of parts to each other and, despite the transcendent promise of the title, the feeling that the realm of the spirit is a false abstraction and repudiation of life, for 'My voice could not carry to you did you dwell in stars.' The voice, or its limitations, is also the constant theme of the final poem, 'Harvest Song'.

I am a reaper whose muscles set at sundown. All my oats are

cradled.
But I am too chilled, and too fatigued to bind them. And I
hunger.

I crack a grain between my teeth. I do not taste it.
I have been in the fields all day. My throat is dry. I hunger
(p. 69).

The pastoral setting is betrayed by images of exhaustion and the kind
of drought that featured in 'November Cotton Flower'. The speaker
says he is blind, yet he seeks the 'stack'd fields of other harvesters' but
fears to call to them. His ears too are 'caked with dust of oatfields at
harvest-time' making him deaf; his throat is dry, and despite the field
holler which denoted community and struggle in 'Cotton Song,' the
sun has gone down on him: 'Now that the sun has set and I am chilled,
I fear to call. (Eoho, my brothers!)' With a dry throat and caked ears
the speaker would find it difficult to call, or to hear the response—and
it is exactly the failure of the call and response form which gives this,
Cane's final poem, such a bleak message of isolation and distress. In
a letter to Waldo Frank describing the movement of the book Toomer
wrote that Cane 'ends (pauses) in Harvest Song,' implying that the
work's final statement should be one of alienation and loss. But in the
same letter he stated that 'the curve really starts with Bona and Paul
(awakening),'[1] suggesting that what became the final story in Cane's
second part might hold a clue to work's inception.

'Bona and Paul' is a semi-autobiographical story in four parts, set
in Chicago, where Toomer had lived, worked and enrolled in a physical training college in 1916.[2] It is probably the first story that Toomer
wrote, and it is the only one in Cane set in almost exclusively 'white'
environments. The story opens in a gymnasium, where Paul Johnson,
a mixed-race student from the south, is 'drilling' with other students
who 'are going to be teachers' in order to train 'sick people who all
their lives have been drilling' (p.70).The theme of restraint through
social convention appears immediately here, and Paul is established
as something of an outsider in that he is momentarily 'out of step'

1   *Brother Mine: The Correspondence of Jean Toomer and Waldo Frank*, p. 86.
2   Byrd and Gates, 'Song of the Son', p. xli.

with the other drilling students. The focus of the story shifts to the erotic and physical interaction between Paul and Bona, a southern white girl who watches Paul moving: 'Bona: He is a harvest moon. He is an autumn leaf. He is a nigger. Bona! But don't all the dorm girls say so? And don't you, when you are sane, say so? That's why I love—Oh, nonsense.' In thoughts and words that echo Bob Stone's racially conflicted love for Louisa in 'Blood Burning Moon' ('it was because she was nigger that he went to her') Bona's fascination with Paul emerges. She joins in a game of basketball, Paul accidentally strikes her on the jaw and catches and holds her; she is surprised and angry, but suddenly 'a new passion flares at him and makes her stomach fall' (p. 71), and she runs from the hall.

The second part opens with Paul looking through the two windows of his room, and deploying the light and dark imagery that featured in 'Theater,' the narrator states 'Bona is one window. One window, Paul.' Through 'his' window he looks at the setting sun:

> Paul follows the sun to a pine-matted hillock in Georgia … A Negress chants a lullaby beneath the mate-eyes of a southern planter. Her breasts are ample for the suckling of a song.

Paul looks out onto a scene of his own 'miscegenated' birth, and the nurturing spirit of the south produces a song, *Cane*'s symbol of culture and belonging. He turns to look through Bona's window but finds that he merely 'looks through a dark pane.' Paul's roommate Art, like Bona, also muses about Paul's ethnic identity, explaining Paul's apparent moodiness by concluding 'It's his blood. Dark Blood … Nigger?' (p. 72), and Art makes it clear that Paul is actually 'passing' for white when he wishes Paul would 'only come out, one way or the other, and tell a feller' (p. 75). Paul and Art have dates. They go to a restaurant, then go to meet the girls, and while they wait Art starts to play jazz piano. 'The picture of Our Poets hung perilously' (p. 73) the narrator states, as popular culture starts to undercut the kind of school-room portraits of past Literary Greats that decorate the walls. At the same time, the jazz piano starts Paul musing about ethnic characteristics—and the symbolism of light and dark. Paul thinks about getting Art to play jazz 'in the daytime' when Art might be 'more himself,' or, curiously, 'More Nigger. Different?' Perhaps 'white skins are not supposed to live at night,' thinks Paul, but then decides that Bona wouldn't be pale, although he isn't sure.

Such ambiguous interior reflections on racial characteristics, art and emotion, actually clarify the story's central theme, which isn't the essential nature of race and character, but the inherent ambiguity of 'race' itself. Bona and Helen accompany the men to a nightclub, and on the way the asphalt boulevards seem to 'resemble Negro shanties in some southern alley' (p. 73). Bona tells Paul she loves him, but he hesitates in returning the compliment and this drives a temporary wedge between them. When they enter the nightclub Paul is aware of stares and speculation about his race, and 'A strange thing happened to Paul. Suddenly he knew that he was apart from the people around him. Apart from the pain ... he knew that people saw, not attractiveness in his dark skin, but difference' (p. 74). The band play jazz and the singer sings, and Paul's thoughts still move around ideas of race, but he moves towards the 'dark pane' of Bona, and the music re-invokes a negress who 'chants a lullaby beneath the mate-eyes of a southern planter,' and this causes Paul and Bona to connect again, as he promises Bona that she will know 'The truth of what I was thinking ... before the evening's over' (p.76). Spiteful and racist thoughts about Paul feature in Helen's thoughts, although she too seems secretly fascinated by him. Some comments Helen makes cause tension to arise between Bona and Paul, but after a confused and sarcastic exchange, he holds her and 'Passionate blood leaps back into their eyes .... They know that the pink-faced people have no part in what they feel' (p. 77). They head for the exit and some kind of consummation, past the 'big uniformed black man who opens and closes the gilded exit door;' but 'As the black man swings the door for them, his eyes are knowing.' The doorman's silent insinuation initiates a bizarre vision for Paul out in the night air; he sees the nightclub 'purple,' and as if he were far off, 'And a spot is in the purple. The spot comes furiously towards him. Face of the black man. It leers. It smiles sweetly like a child's.' Paul turns back to the doorman:

'You're wrong.'

'Yassur.'

'Brother, you're wrong.

'I came back to tell you, to shake your hand, and tell you that you are wrong. That something beautiful is going to happen … That I danced with her, and did not know her. That I felt passion, contempt and passion for her whom I did not know … That my thoughts were matches thrown into a dark window. And all the while the Gardens were purple like a bed of roses would be at dusk. I came back to tell you, brother, that white faces are petals of roses. That dark faces are petals of dusk. That I am going out and gather petals. That I am going out and know her whom I brought here with me to these Gardens which are purple like a bed of roses would be at dusk' (pp. 77-8).

Paul's language deploys some of the metaphors that the story has used in its meditations on race and colour—windows, colours, flowers and petals—and as he finally shakes the doorman's hand the reader can only wonder what effect this had on the man. Literary convention might suggest that Paul's lyrical attempt to communicate his determination to know and love his partner would trigger some sympathy or recognition in his listener, and outline a development that here, at the end of *Cane*'s second subdivision, would resolve some of the work's tensions and lighten the bleakness of its atmosphere. But the final line of the story comes like a slap in the face, for when Paul 'reached the spot where they had been standing, Bona was gone' (p. 78).

Like the narrator of 'Avey', Paul has misread a situation and been blinded by his own dreams. The reconciliation with Bona has failed; but more ominously the reconciliation of the racial groups has failed, and ethnic and sexual taboos and boundaries, even in the modern northern city, seem to stubbornly resist subversion. But *Cane* doesn't end here. It ends with the extended drama 'Kabnis' which, in many ways, will add another complicating section to the 'arc' of *Cane* by bringing the reader full circle. 'Kabnis' will present the trials of a northern artist living in the south, showing him grappling with the experiences which will enable—or compel—him to find words which will allow him to be 'the face of the South' (p. 81). What the final section of *Cane* presents to the reader is an artist struggling to find the words that will eventually become a book like *Cane*.

4.3 Kabnis: The Return to the South

The final subdivision of *Cane* is, again, semi-autobiographical. Ralph Kabnis is a mixed-race teacher, raised in the north, who has travelled to Georgia to teach and connect with his southern ancestry, much as Toomer had done in 1921. As Nellie McKay writes, Kabnis is someone,

> who stands at a historical and cultural crossroads in search of a meaningful explanation of his own being in time and place. His journey toward that goal incorporates the fears, alienation, ambivalence, and the sense of oppressive control by others that are a part of the heritage of the black experience in white America.[1]

That such a condition expressed something of Toomer's own situation is certain. Toomer wrote to Waldo Frank as *Cane* progressed stating 'Kabnis is *Me*,'[2] and although this is not a literal statement it is a declaration that in 'Kabnis' Toomer was self-reflexively dramatising his own to attempts to express his experiences in literary form.

The drama opens in a shack, with Ralph Kabnis, neurotic and sleepless, trying to read in bed. His skin tone announces his mixed ancestry—'Brown eyes stare from a lemon face'—as he listens to the Georgia winds and 'the weird chill of their song:

> White-man's land.
> Niggers, sing.
> Burn, bear black children
> Till poor rivers bring
> Rest, and sweet glory
> In Camp Ground (p. 81).

This snatch of sorrow song isn't heard but could be 'composed' by Kabnis as he nervously listens to the wind. The lyric will reappear

1 McKay, *Jean Toomer, Artist*, pp. 151–2.
2 *Brother Mine: The Correspondence of Jean Toomer and Waldo Frank*, p. 102.

three times as the winds bear this pitiless message of black fortune into the text, and Kabnis' interior monologue makes it clear at the outset that he is an artist longing for the oracle of the south to give him words:

> Kabnis: Near me. Now. Whoever you are, my warm glowing sweetheart .... Ralph Kabnis is a dream. And dreams are faces with large eyes and weak chins and broad brows that get smashed by the fists of square faces. The body of the world is bull-necked ... God, if I could develop that in words .... If I could feel that I came to the South to face it. If I, the dream (not what is weak and afraid in me) could become the face of the South. How my lips would sing for it, my songs being the lips of its soul. Soul. Soul hell. There aint no such thing. What in hell was that?

The dream to become the lips of the south's soul is disturbed by a rat whose movements spray Kabnis with the red 'Dust of slavefields' (p. 82), 'baptising' him with southern soil. Kabnis has imagined the south as a bull-necked oppressor, smashing his dream; he is so agitated that he pulls the head from noisy chicken whose cackling has angered him and throws it out into the Georgia night—which inaugurates a description of 'the serene loveliness of Georgian autumn moonlight,' and a reappearance of the pine smoke which suffused the first part of *Cane*: 'down in the valley, a band of pine-smoke, silvered gauze, drifts steadily.' Oscillating between beauty and horror—as Toomer had said of his own work, 'saturate with the pain and joy, the ugliness and beauty of a peasant people'—the narrative takes the moon and transforms it into a white baby; the wind serenades it with a lullaby which recalls the negress who had sung to her child 'beneath the mate-eyes of a southern planter' in 'Bona and Paul:'

> rock a-by baby . .
> Black mother sways, holding a white child on her bosom.
> when the bough bends . .
> Her breath hums through pine-cones.
> cradle will fall . .
> Teat moon-children at your breasts,
> down will come baby . .

Black mother.

The montage of nursery rhyme, miscegenation and calamity ('down will come baby') emphasises the gothic horror of the south, but again, the night's beauty arises, literally prostrating the protagonist and exposing the conflict he feels:

> He looks up, and the night's beauty strikes him dumb. He falls to his knees. Sharp stones cut through his thin pajamas …
> 'God Almighty, dear God, dear Jesus, do not torture me with beauty. Take it away. Give me an ugly world. Ha, ugly. Stinking like unwashed niggers. Dear Jesus, do not chain me to myself and set these hills and valleys, heaving with folk-songs, so close to me that I cannot reach them' (p. 83).

Kabnis' breakdown personifies and dramatises *Cane*'s central theme: a yearning for the south and the sense of 'being in time and place' that its apparent rootedness and community promises. But all Kabnis can do is gaze past the school buildings to the town's court house tower and imagine himself lynched there: 'He sees himself yanked beneath that tower. He sees white minds, with indolent assumption, juggle justice and a nigger ….' Feeling he is going mad, Kabnis panics, looking for ghosts, but eventually he falls asleep while the wind chants 'White-man's land. / Niggers, sing' as the first scene ends.

Part of Kabnis' distress is caused by his hatred for his employer, Samuel Hanby, the principal who runs the school on doctrines derived from the educational philosophy of Booker T. Washington, an influential orator and advisor to American presidents at the turn of the century who preached accommodation and black consent to a lack of civil rights in exchange for patronage from businessmen and industrialists. Such an ideology of 'economic progress and political quietism,'[1] extolling patience, thrift and respectability—narrow bourgeois values—had been parodied by Toomer in *Cane*'s earlier sections. For Kabnis this means that he can't drink and can only furtively smoke on the 'school property' of his run-down cabin—his

---

1   Scruggs and Vandemarr, *Jean Toomer and the Terrors of American History*, p. 42.

predicament ironically suggests the conditions of slave quarters—
and this makes him look forward to seeing his friends Fred Halsey
and 'Professor'[1] Layman. Part two opens in Halsey's parlour. As the
photographs in Halsey's room stress, he, like most of *Cane*'s characters, is of mixed racial heritage; his great grandfather is 'an English
gentleman,' his great grandmother bears just a trace of the 'Negro
strain,' his father is 'rich brown' and his mother 'practically white.'
Halsey and Layman, who is by turns 'teacher and preacher' (p. 86),
give Kabnis a cautionary lesson in the ways of the south, as it is
Kabnis' 'first time out' down there. The talk soon turns to lynching, and in the teeth of Kabnis' proposition that such things wouldn't
happen to 'men like us three here,' Layman insists 'Nigger's a nigger
down this away, Professor. An only two dividins: good and bad. An
even they aint permanent categories' (p. 86), as they can be easily
mixed up when it comes to lynching.

Kabnis bemoans the fact that black Americans are a 'preacher-rid-
den race' (p.88) as the singing from the nearby church gets louder,
and aligns himself with the people of the town who called such serv-
ices 'shouting,' saying that up north: 'In the church I used to go to on
one ever shouted' (89). The southerners gently mock Kabnis for his
'dictie' ways, and the talk shifts to Lewis, another black visitor from
the north, and another semi-autobiographical portrait of Toomer himself. Lewis, however, is more politically outspoken than Kabnis, and
seems to represent a threat to the town's uneasy racial concord. As if
to reinforce this, the friends tell Kabnis about the lynching of Mame
Lamkins, a woman who hid her husband from the mob; as a result she
was murdered, her still living foetus torn from her belly and impaled
by a knife that 'stuck it t a tree' (p. 90).[2] Just as Layman finishes this
account, a shriek of 'Jesus, Jesus, I've found Jesus' comes from the
church, and at the same time a stone with a message wrapped around
it crashes through the window. Kabnis is terrified, and the note that
reads 'You northern nigger, its time fer y t leave' sends him over the

1   'Professor' is a respectful term for any educated person, teacher, preacher or
    musician.
2   Toomer changes the details here, but this is essentially an account of the lynch-
    ing of a black woman called Mary Turner in 1915.

edge. He dashes from the room, his friends follow, and the church choir sings 'My Lord, what a mourning. / When the stars begin to fall' (p.91), echoing 'Blood Burning Moon's premonition of the final judgement.

The third scene finds Kabnis delirious with fear. Halsey and Layman try to calm him down, clean him up, and convince him that the threatening note wasn't meant for him, and didn't come from white people. As Halsey says, 'White folks aint in fer all them theatrics these days' (p. 92), and had they wanted Kabnis they would have just come right in and taken him. They are giving Kabnis a drink when Hanby, the school principal enters, and patronisingly fires Kabnis, pontificating that 'the progress of the Negro race is jeopardised whenever the personal habits and examples set by its guides and mentors fall below the acknowledged and hard-won standard of its average member' (p. 93). Halsey salvages Kabnis' pride by retorting that it was already fixed that 'He's goin t work with me' in his workshop, 'Shapin shafts and buildin wagons'll make a man of him what nobody … can take advantage of' (p. 94).

The irony that an educated man from the north has failed at educating the south and will now be working in an the outdated profession of wagon-building, doesn't seem to be lost on Kabnis, as from here to the end of the drama he is a bitter man. As if to balance his character, Lewis, the other northern visitor, enters the scene, and is described as 'what a stronger Kabnis might have been' (p. 95). The group talk, and Lewis reveals that the threatening note was meant for him, as 'Some Negroes have become uncomfortable at my being here.' What is hinted at as Lewis' questioning of the townsfolk, his criticisms of southern conduct and his political agenda, has upset the locals, and this institutes both a contrast and a connection between Kabnis the bitter artist and Lewis the reformer. A vision is produced when their eyes meet. Kabnis is imaged as 'uprooted,' 'Suspended a few feet above the soil whose touch would resurrect him.' Kabnis feels a need to rush into Lewis' arms and to call him 'Brother,' but his cynicism wins, Kabnis' lip curls, and the connection is lost.

A month has passed when scene four opens. In Halsey's workshop Lewis is criticising the hold that religion has on the population. Kabnis asks why he didn't come to 'us professors' to get an opinion of the south, but Lewis says of Kabnis, enigmatically, that 'Life has already told him more than he is capable of knowing' (p. 99). Lewis turns to Halsey, who he says 'Fits here' and is 'an artist' in his way; Halsey agrees, saying that he has been to France, been to the north, and been to school, 'but there aint no books whats got th feel t them of them there tools. Nassur.' The contrast with the rootless Kabnis is stark, and is reinforced when a white man comes in to have the handle of a hatchet fixed; Kabnis attempts the job but botches it in front of the customer, and feels 'the whole white South weighs down upon him' (p. 100). Halsey's young sister, Carrie K., eases the tension when she arrives carrying lunch. As well as food for the Kabnis and her brother, she has some for an old man who lives down in the workshop's cellar. She is about to take it down to him when her attention is drawn to Lewis, and a moment of revelation occurs as 'Their meeting is a swift sunburst' (p. 101). Lewis, like many of the narrators in *Cane*, has a vision prompted by a desired woman: 'his mind flashes images of her life in the southern town,' and fears to see 'Her rich beauty fading' there. He looks at her with 'Christ eyes' and for her part 'Fearlessly she loves into them.' But then Carrie K. is assaulted by the repression of convention as 'The sin-bogies of respectable southern colored folks' command her to be 'a *good* girl' and, gaining control of herself, she marches 'rigidly' downstairs to feed the old man. Here, the conflict between desire and repression is played out, alongside the often eroticised but baffled wish to possess the beauty of the south: Lewis 'wants to take her North with him. What for?' (p. 102)—neither he nor the text can tell us.

Halsey reminds Lewis that there will be a get-together that night, and the scene ends. Scene five opens with a lyrical invocation that recaps the south's mythic themes:

> Night, soft belly of a pregnant Negress, throbs evenly against the torso of the South. Night throbs a womb-song to the South. Cane and cotton-fields, pine forests, cypress swamps, saw-mills, and factories are fecund at her touch (p. 103).

The final appearance of the 'White-man's land. / Niggers, sing' lyric then introduces the town at night, and witnesses Halsey, Lewis, Kabnis and two women, Stella and Cora, enter Halsey's workshop and descend into the cellar or 'the Hole' beneath it. Down there is the old man or 'Father,' 'Gray-bearded. Gray-haired. Prophetic. Immobile;' Lewis sees him as 'A mute John the Baptist of a new religion—or a tongue-tied shadow of an old;' the narrator calls him a 'Slave boy … Moses …. Dead blind father of a muted folk'[1] (p. 104). The old man's ancient grandeur personifies a heritage and promises answers that fascinate Lewis; but the old man's mumbling enrages Kabnis. Despite his inarticulacy, it will be the old man who becomes the 'oracle' whose pronouncements describe the last arc of *Cane*'s narrative.

The women, Cora and Stella, are 'good time girls', but their descriptions reflect the pain of black history and experience: Cora is 'a tall, thin, mulatto woman,' and Stella is a 'brown-skin girl' who laughs with a twisted mouth that betrays 'the life she's been through.' (p. 105). She says later that 'a white man took m mother' (p. 107) and it broke her father's heart; since then she doesn't care what becomes of her, and all the men she has known have been 'Boars an kids an fools.' Another woman was expected at the party, but when Halsey asks 'Wheres Clover Stel?' he learns that her Jim is drunk and 'Said he'd bust her head open if she went out' (pp. 105–6). In a series of asides the drama conveys the lot of southern black women: living for stolen pleasures, but suffering brutal treatment—not least because they bear the brunt of the racial subjugation their menfolk suffer. As Halsey explains to Lewis, 'Th nigger hates th sight of a black woman worse than death. Sorry t mix y up this way, Lewis' (p. 106).

The group are amused at Lewis' confusion and outrage on hearing about such cycles of cruelty, and eventually the party starts,

---

1   Toomer's play 'Balo', written around 1921–22, presents a similar character in an old, blind, ex-slave called Uncle Ned, an ancient and saintly 'Negro prophet' who embodies the origins of the folk community that the play celebrates. See Toomer, 'Balo,' in James V. Hatch and Ted Shine (eds), *Black Theatre USA: Plays by African Americans 1847 to Today* (New York and London: The Free Press, 1996), pp. 223–30, p. 228.

grotesquely, with Kabnis putting on an old gaudy robe 'with great mock-solemnity' (p. 105). Kabnis' self-alienation is emphasised by this act, as he is 'a curious spectacle, acting a part, yet very real.' Lewis is surprised, and laughs, but Kabnis just regards him with 'furtive hatred' as the drinking starts. Lewis continues to look at Kabnis and a row erupts as Kabnis objects to Lewis' 'godam nosin' (p. 106). Lewis admonishes him with the old man, insisting on 'The old man as symbol, flesh, and spirit of the past, what do you think he would say if he could see you?' But Kabnis denies his slave past, saying his ancestors 'were Southern blue-bloods,' and Lewis rebukes the shallowness of Kabnis' denial by twisting the knife in his weaknesses: 'Cant hold them, can you? Master; slave. Soil; and the overarching heavens. Dusk; dawn. They fight and bastardize you.' The acidic power of Lewis' taunt is lost, however, as Stella starts to tell Lewis about her tragic life and Kabnis, rejected by Stella, starts to pay attention to Cora.

It is then Halsey's turn to tell Lewis his story; however, sensing that the talk has turned to him, Kabnis returns to the table and, his tongue loosened by alcohol, makes a drunken statement about his poetic vocation that actually functions as a summary of *Cane*'s aesthetics. Kabnis claims that he was born an 'orator' and mocks the crudity of Halsey's manual profession while declaiming that since the cradle,

> I've been shapin words after a design that branded here. Know whats here? M soul. Ever heard o that? ... Been shapin words t fit m soul ... I've been shapin words; ah, but sometimes theyre beautiful an golden an have a taste that makes them fine t roll over with y tongue ....
>
> ... Those words I was tellin y about, they wont fit int th mold thats branded on m soul. Rhyme, y see? Poet, too. Bad rhyme. Bad poet. Somethin else youve learned tnight. Lewis dont know it all, an I'm atellin y. Ugh. Th form thats burned int my soul is some twisted awful thing that crept in from a dream, a godam nightmare, an wont stay still unless I feed it. An it lives on

words. Not beautiful words. God Almighty no. Misshapen, split-
gut, tortured, twisted words … I want t feed the soul … I wish t
God some lynchin white man ud stick his knife through it an pin
it to a tree (p. 109).

Kabnis the artist has been shaping words to contain 'a meaningful
explanation of his own being in time and place,' and sometimes
these words are beautiful. But often they don't 'rhyme' with his
soul, because, as he had declared at the opening of the drama, 'The
body of the world is bull-necked' and turns his dreams into violent
nightmares. The only language left is comprised of 'Misshapen, split-
gut, tortured, twisted words' which will, in a horrible resurrection of
an image from the lynching of Mame Lamkins, pin his soul, or the
awful aborted thing that has replaced it, to a tree. Kabnis' conclusion
is that 'This whole damn bloated purple country' is 'goin down t hell
in a holy avalanche of words.'

In 1923, before *Cane*'s publication, Toomer had written to Claude
Barnett of the Associated Negro Press that 'My style, my esthetic, is
nothing more nor less than my attempt to fashion my substance into
works of art,'[1] but the violent tensions and frustrations in the themes
and language of the finished work suggest his 'substance' was more
intractable than he had led others to believe. Kabnis' rant about 'tortured, twisted words' doesn't describe the poetics and aesthetics of
Cane very accurately, but it does expose the despair that lies at the
heart of the work. It also sparks a sudden development in the action.
After Kabnis' outburst, Cora squeezes his head into her breasts;
Stella looks on jealously, but Halsey grabs her and starts kissing her.
Lewis 'finds himself completely cut out,' feels the weight of the town
descend upon him, and, despite being the one character that seemed
to embody the hope of social justice, reason, change and reform, he
finds the characters' pain 'too intense. He cannot stand it. He bolts
from the table. Leaps up the stairs. Plunges through the work-shop
and out into the night' (p. 110), taking any promise of redemption that
Cane's pages contain with him.

The final scene opens with the cellar swimming in the 'pale phos-

---

1   *The Letters of Jean Toomer 1919–1924*, p. 160.

phorescence' of a post-debauch morning. Halsey wakes them up and Kabnis complains, only half-ironically, that 'its preposterous t root an artist out o bed at this ungodly hour.' In a last flicker of mythic vision, the narrative describes the waking women as 'two princesses in Africa going through the early morning ablutions of their pagan prayers' (p. 111), but at this point the text seems too exhausted for such indulgences. The women leave, and Kabnis turns his attention to the old man, who has to bear the brunt of his disillusion. The old man is, as Lewis had said, a 'symbol, flesh, and spirit of the past,' but the past won't give up its meanings to Kabnis—or gives him only its dreams of gothic horror—so he demythologises the old man, stripping him of his symbolism by reifying his situation: 'Do y think youre out of slavery? Huh? Youre where they used t throw th worked-out, no-count slaves. On a damp clammy floor of a dark scum-hole' (p. 112). Carrie K. brings down the old man's food, and suddenly the old man says and repeats the word 'Sin.' Kabnis scoffs at the old man, declaring that 'he doesnt know what he's talkin about. Couldnt know. It was only a preacher's sin they knew in those old days, an that wasnt sin at all' (p. 114). Kabnis uses himself as the benchmark of sin and suffering: 'Th whole world is a conspiracy t sin, especially in America, an against me. I'm th victim of their sin. I'm what sin is. Does he look like me?' What Kabnis implies is that he is a product of a heritage of slavery, miscegenation and rootlessness, which gives his condition and his suffering a modern caste that previous generations can't understand. He is probably both wrong and fantastically egotistical here, but we are meant to sympathise with him: the nature of black American anguish has changed, but, *Cane* seems to imply, it has not lessened.

Finally the old man utters more than isolated words: 'Th sin whats fixed … upon th white folks,', 'f tellin Jesus—lies. O th sin th white folks 'mitted when they made th Bible lie.' The oracle of the past, of black history and culture, has spoken with its broken voice. But Kabnis is scornful: 'So thats your sin. All these years t tell us that th white folks made th Bible lie. Well, I'll be damned. Lewis ought t have been here. You old black fakir …' (p.115). These are the last words that Kabnis utters before ascending the stairs to a job he has no aptitude for in an occupation whose days are numbered. Left alone, Carrie K. goes to the old man and kneels, whispering 'Jesus, come;' 'light streaks through the iron-barred cellar window' and frames them, and *Cane*'s final lines look to the birth of a new dawn:

> Outside, the sun arises from its cradle in the tree-tops of the forest. Shadows of pines are dreams the sun shakes from its eyes. The sun arises. Gold-glowing child, it steps into the sky and sends a birth-song slanting down gray dust streets and sleepy windows of the southern town.

Lewis has fled from the pain of the town, Kabnis is working at a doomed job and wishing a lyncher would impale his soul, and Carrie K. is waiting for a sign from the oracle of black history—an oracle which, as *Cane*'s twenty-nine montaged stories, lyrics and poems have shown us, has saturated its messages with the blood and toil, the songs and sufferings, the pain and joy and the ugliness and beauty of the black American experience, but has left us no answers. The dawn and gold-glowing child of the last scene comes too late to redeem any of the book's characters, but as Toomer had insisted, '*Cane* was a swan-song. It was a song of an end.' It wasn't, however, a song of a resolution or completion. Complementing the isolated arcs that graphically introduce each section, *Cane* remains the archetypal modernist text: fragmented and dynamic, beautiful and enigmatic, but like history itself, never finished, and often unfulfilled.

5. *Cane* and Criticism

The reviews and criticism that *Cane* attracted on its appearance were on the whole positive, and the most important of these early reviews are included in the collection of critical essays, letters and extracts from Toomer's autobiographical writings that appear in the Norton Critical Editions of *Cane* (1988 and 2011). Early reviewers tended to acclaim *Cane*'s experimentalism even if its message left them perplexed. In a lengthy review in *Opportunity* (1923) Montgomery Gregory lauded *Cane*'s use of folk culture, its avoidance of standard literary conventions and forms, and its combination of 'the inheritance of the old Negro and the spirit of the new Negro.'[1] As has been noted, in the *Crisis* (1924) W .E. B. du Bois praised *Cane*'s courage in challenging the 'sex conventionality' (p. 184) of modern writing, even while he criticised the apparent obscurity of some of its meanings. As already noted, even the more critical reviews, such as Robert Littell's in the *New Republic* (1923) praised Cane's originality, calling it 'an interesting, occasionally beautiful and often queer book of exploration' (p. 183).

Early reviews, including less approving ones from the *New York Tribune* and *Boston Transcript* in 1923, are collected in the first critical anthology dedicated to Toomer's work—and the first book-length volume on him *per se*—the *Merrill Studies in 'Cane,'* edited by Frank Durham (1971). Renewed interest in *Cane* in the second half of the twentieth century had been prompted by the conscious-ness-raising projects of the 1960s and the rise of African-American studies in the academy. In 1968 'Karintha', 'Blood Burning Moon,' and four poems, three of them from *Cane*, were anthologised in the

---

1   Jean Toomer, *Cane*, second Norton edition, edited by Byrd and Gates Jr, p. 178.

popular New American Library paperback *Black Voices*,[1] and the appearance of a new paperback edition of *Cane* followed in 1969. Durham's *Studies in 'Cane'* rode the wave of this interest, and carried new critical essays as well as early reviews and extracts from books such as Robert A. Bone's *The Negro Novel in America* (1958), which emphasised the fact that apart from brief treatments in such surveys of black American literature, *Cane* had received very little critical attention between the late 1920s and early 1970s. Durham's collection contains Waldo Frank's 1923 introduction to *Cane*, and Arna Bontemps introduction to the 1969 paperback, and rather unnecessarily groups its other material into the categories of 'Black Reviewers' and 'White Reviewers' and repeats this compartmentalisation for the critical essays—a distinction made doubly superfluous by the fact that Durham mistakenly put two white writers into the black category.[2]

Durham's collection contains some interesting pieces of criticism which don't concern *Cane* but highlight some of the social and racial strictures that Toomer was subject to. 'The Only Negro Member of the Poetry Society of South Carolina' is written by Durham himself, and documents the mortification felt by the society upon discovering that one of their members was a person 'of colour' and in 1923 was about to publish a book 'nationally advertised as 'a book about negroes by a negro.''[3] Whether Toomer was aware—or indeed cared—about the society's embarrassment is unrecorded, but the Poetry Society of South Carolina avoided scandal by retaining Toomer's name on its membership list but excluding *Cane* from the list of 'books by members' included in its yearbook. Another interesting contextual piece in Durham's collection is a report from *Time* magazine (March 28. 1932) entitled 'Just Americans,' which opens with the statement 'No Negro can legally marry a white woman in any Southern State' (p. 15). It goes on to relate that Toomer had married Marjorie Latimer in California, that Toomer was 'an exponent of Georges Gurdjieff,

---

1   Abraham Chapman (ed.), *Black Voices: An Anthology of Afro-American Literature* (New York: New American Library, 1968).
2   See W. Edward Farrison, 'Jean Toomer's *Cane* Again' (1972), reprinted in Jean Toomer, *Cane*, first Norton edition, edited by Turner, pp. 175–80, pp. 175–7.
3   Frank Durham,(ed.), *The Merrill Studies in 'Cane'* (Columbus: Charles E. Merrill Publishing, 1971) , p. 11.

the Armenian-Greek cultist,' and that he conducted racially and sexually 'mixed' study groups that shared 'unconventional' living and
sleeping arrangements in order to, in Toomer's quoted words, 'eradi-
cate the false veneer of civilization with its unnatural inhibitions ...
and unnatural behaviour.' The overtones of miscegenation in *Time*'s
report would haunt Toomer, consolidating an aversion to publicity
which helped with his post-*Cane* 'disappearance' but also, more trag-
ically, perhaps contributed to the tragic death of his wife in child-
birth—it has been suggested that despite complications both parents
had insisted on a home delivery because of their fear of the press
attention a hospital birth would generate.[1] The *Time* piece does, however, allow space for Toomer's radical claims about American racial
destiny: ' ... there are no racial barriers any more, because there are
so many Americans with strains of Negro, Indian and Oriental blood
.... They will not be white, black or yellow—just Americans.'[2]

Durham's collection also contains an extract from Mabel Mayle
Dillard's unpublished (1967) PhD thesis on Toomer, which liberally
cites excerpts from Fisk University's collection of Toomer's letters
and manuscripts—materials which would become familiar features of
Toomer exegesis from this point on. Dillard's thesis would also provide the basis for the first full-length study of Toomer's work, Brian
Joseph Benson and Mabel Mayle Dillard's, *Jean Toomer* (1980).[3]
Their study borrows the metaphor of the 'veil' of black American
experience from the writings of W. E. B. du Bois ('the Negro is a
sort of seventh son, born with a veil, and gifted with second-sight in
this American world') which also appeared in a letter from the black
editor Claude Barnett in April 1923, who without knowing Toomer's
ethnic heritage had stated ' ... how else could you interpret 'us' as

---

1 Charles R. Larson, *Invisible Darkness: Jean Toomer and Nella Larsen* (Iowa:
University of Iowa Press, 1993), p. 133.
2 Durham, *The Merrill Studies in 'Cane'*, p. 16.
3 By this time there was a considerable amount of articles and book chapters that
dealt with Toomer's work, and Benson and Dillard's study includes an exhaus-
tively annotated bibliography.

you do unless you had peeked behind the veil?'[1] The first chapter, 'Behind the Veil: Jean Toomer's Progression,' uses letters and auto-biographical writings to outline Toomer's life, emphasising the racial mixing that featured in both his family and formative environments, the literary and artistic influences that shaped his own work, and his later involvement with Gurdjieff's teachings and the Society of Friends. 'Lifting the Veil: *Cane*' follows, providing a section-by-section discussion of the work and giving interesting insights into key textual features like shifting points of view and Toomer's imagistic or 'poetic' prose. Benson and Dillard don't shy away from the difficulty or extreme openness of interpretation that readers of *Cane* often face; in fact, they propose that it is a key aspect of Toomer's aesthetic program:

> Toomer ... believed that poetry ought to encompass a new type of language ... the language and ideas of poetry ought to be necessarily obscure and only hint at partial revelation. His method of partial revelation is readily seen in his poetry and throughout *Cane*.[2]

Following their own insights, Benson and Dillard refuse to view 'Kabnis' as a 'completion' of *Cane*, or—and this will be a touchstone for differing interpretations—glimpse any sense of redemption in this final section. For them, the work's beauty 'lies with the fading 'song-lit' race' of the book's first subdivision, while its final scenes merely present a modern young man's 'tragic collapse,' wherein 'the protagonist slowly loses his sense of self-direction and lapses into self-hatred and indolence' (p. 95).

The next chapter, titled 'The Veil Replaced,' looks in detail at Toomer's resistance to racial categorisation, and underlines the fact that it would be an ideal of racial fusion 'to which he devoted his final literary efforts' (p.108). The next chapter discusses some of these literary pieces, including the stories 'Easter,' 'Winter on Earth,' 'Mr

---

1   Cited in Benson and Dillard, *Jean Toomer*, p. 33. Toomer would answer ' ... your contention is sustained. I have 'peeped behind the veil," in a letter of April 29, 1923 (*The Letters of Jean Toomer 1919–1924*, p. 160).

2   Benson and Dillard, *Jean Toomer*, p. 37.

Costyve Duditch,' and his long poem 'The Blue Meridian.' As they point out, the prose pieces, although experimental, are nothing like *Cane*'s prose, but act as polemical if obscure parables about modern life and its spiritual bankruptcy. The theme of African-American experience is entirely absent from these prose pieces, but it returns in poetic form in 'The Blue Meridian' as an attempt to fuse his own early concerns with racial intermingling and American identity with his later focus on spiritual growth and transcendence. Benson and Dillard's conclusions set the tone of most subsequent assessments of Toomer's literary career: *Cane*'s brilliance shines all the more brightly because of the thinness of his later output. After 1923, Toomer had 'lost touch' with both the world of literature and the creative impulses which had produced his early work, and many would agree with Benson and Dillard when they wrote that there 'has been nothing like *Cane* before or since. Our judgement of Jean Toomer must rest with this admission' (p. 132).

In 1982 *The Wayward and the Seeking: A Collection of Writings by Jean Toomer* edited by Darwin W. Turner was published, giving access to a wide range of published and unpublished autobiographical sketches, short fictions, poetry and drama. These writings, especially the autobiographical pieces, would become central to Toomer criticism, although recent critics have warned about taking the material selected for *The Wayward and the Seeking* as a wholly accurate account of Toomer's life and its contexts, as editorial selection as well as authorial omissions and misrepresentations need to be taken into account.[1]

Nellie Y. McKay's *Jean Toomer, Artist: A Study of His Literary Life and Work, 1894–1936* appeared in 1984, and provided an accessible and insightful analysis of Toomer's life, his writing and its contexts. McKay's early chapters focus on Toomer's life and development as an artist, and illustrate his early concern with racial politics and African-American folk culture through close readings of the plays *Balo* and *Natalie Mann*. This sets the stage for her discussion of

---

1   Scruggs and Vandemarr, *Jean Toomer and the Terrors of American History*, pp. 5–6.

Cane, which receives extended treatment (a chapter for each subdivision) through nuanced readings of the work's politics. McKay uses issues of gender, authority and appropriation, for example, to analyse the antagonistic relationship between narrator and character in certain sections, and stresses the way in which Toomer's own uncertainties about his identity and his role as artistic recorder of black culture become an integral part of *Cane*'s narrative dynamics:

> Throughout his personal journey for self-definition, Toomer recognised both male and female aspects of himself, and he made frequent use of gender-defined qualities in his characters to explore his relationship to the black folk culture. In 'Fern' and 'Avey,' the male narrator of *Cane* makes his most persistent attempts to claim the black 'female' folk culture as his own. But he does not understand this culture and cannot partake of its nurturing qualities, on one hand, and it refuses to be controlled by male Jean Toomer, representative of the dominant white culture of art and literature, on the other.[1]

McKay presents *Cane*'s sexual politics as problematic, for its female characters often function as mere symbols of nature and sensuality, but she endorses the ways in which *Cane* shows that 'racial and sexual oppression are responsible for the alienation, madness, and death' (p. 91) of the women it portrays, suggesting that in some areas Toomer's attitudes to women and the oppression of their social conditions 'were ahead of his time' (p. 71).

The readings of *Cane*'s subsections in *Jean Toomer, Artist* are meticulously conducted, and focus on the text's related but contradictory themes of cultural celebration, oppression, and historical pessimism. The first subsection ends with Louisa in 'Blood Burning Moon' as a symbol of the tragedy of the south: functioning 'as representation of the folk culture or as woman,' Louisa is 'the final victim' (p. 124) of the brutal forces and changes of the south. McKay finds no solace in the urban section either, seeing its messages as confirmation of 'the discovery by black people that it takes more than

---

1   McKay, *Jean Toomer, Artist*, p. 241.

finding a different place to repair the damage that American slavery and American racial attitudes have wrought on their collective and individual souls' (p. 150). Rather surprisingly, the final moments of 'Kabnis' are held up as images of hope; as the dawn rises over Carrie and Father John in the cellar McKay insists that 'The sun and the new day in positive harmony denote the triumph of *Cane*, which is a portrayal of the union of the past with the present, of the black folk culture with its modern counterpart ... all are part of a whole' (p. 171). What such a reading of these final images actually suggests is the ambiguity and openness of *Cane*'s closing passages—to most critics, rather than giving hope and resolution the ending seems to fall into uncharacteristically conventional symbols of renewal which are undercut by the exhaustion and likely fate of its characters and setting. McKay herself seems to acknowledge this a few pages later when pointing out that the book is 'a work about the pain and struggle wrung from the soul of a people' and a 'confrontation with the meaning of that awful reality' (p. 177). In these closing statements on *Cane* McKay repudiates simplistic readings of even the book's most bucolic moments, and suggests that the work's pessimism is part of its message of struggle: 'In this work, nature is not always associated with beneficence, and Toomer shows that cynicism is often closely associated with survival.'

McKay devotes space to Toomer's Gurdjieff years and the important post-*Cane* publications. She also interrogates his later racial politics intelligently, concluding that America 'on the whole, is not interested in eliminating racial conflict in the lives of Americans,' white America opposes racial intermingling, and black writers are on the whole 'too realistic' to imagine a world in which 'all races are blended into one.' Toomer, however, 'was not willing to accommodate his life and his art to anything else' (p. 240) and in many ways this is the tragedy of his literary career. Toomer's refusal to accommodate anything less than the elimination of racial categories would prompt the title of Alice Walker's essay 'The Divided Life of Jean Toomer' (first published in 1980 and collected in *In Search of Our Mothers' Gardens* in 1983) whose final sentences pinpoint one of the predicaments of Toomer criticism:

> *Cane* was for Toomer a double "swan song." He meant it to
> memorialize a culture he thought was dying, whose folk spirit
> he considered beautiful, but he was also saying good-bye to the
> 'Negro' he felt dying in himself. *Cane* then is a parting gift, and
> no less precious because of that. I think Jean Toomer would want
> us to keep its beauty, but let him go.[1]

Although mildly stated here, Toomer's resistance to racial
categorisation has been regarded by some as the disavowal of a racial
heritage which should rightly have been celebrated, and Walker's high
profile ensured that many readers first encountered Toomer through
this essay and were made aware of the controversy of its author's
racial attitudes at the same time as they discovered his literary output.

Cynthia Earl Kerman and Richard Eldridge's *The Lives of Jean
Toomer: A Hunger for Wholeness* (1987) was the first and up until
now the only attempt to provide a full biography of *Cane*'s author—
although the plural *Lives* of their title hint that their subject's passage
through the world was not a simple one. *The Lives of Jean Toomer*
focuses on Toomer's later spiritual quests and activities—unsurprisingly, as Richard Eldridge was principal of a Quaker school—and
while these are of interest in themselves, the student of *Cane* will be
disappointed that only a quarter of the book's pages are devoted to
Toomer's life and work up to *Cane*'s publication. Subsequent schol-
arship has also pointed out a lot of inaccuracies and omissions in the
biographical methods and materials that the authors employ, com-
pounded by a tendency to take Toomer's own autobiographical testimony as an accurate account of his life.[2] Charles R. Larson's *Invisible
Darkness: Jean Toomer and Nella Larsen* (1993) is also biographical in approach, and in bringing two Harlem Renaissance writers of
mixed race together generates some interesting comparative readings. However, the book's discussion of *Cane* is intermittent, and the
treatment of Toomer tends towards sensationalism in its emphasis on

---

1   Walker, *In Search of Our Mothers' Gardens*, p. 65.
2   See Scruggs and Vandemarr, *Jean Toomer and the Terrors of American History*,
    p. 3, p. 7 and p. 234 note 5.

Toomer's deterioration as a writer after 1923, and as a husband as he fell into self-pity and alcoholism in his later years.

Therman, B. O'Daniel's collection of critical writings, *Jean Toomer: A Critical Evaluation* (1988) is still the largest collection of essays on Toomer's work to date. The volume contains chapters by acknowledged Toomer scholars (Nellie McKay, Darwin T Turner, Mabel Dillard) and collects a wide range of articles which approach Toomer from angles which are still the main points of critical entry into his oeuvre. The essays are organised into sections which include studies of Toomer's life, his relationship with other writers (Waldo Frank, Sherwood Anderson, Hart Crane) and his relationship with Gurdjieff. Toomer's plays and poetry—both within and post-*Cane*—have dedicated sections, but the sections containing essays which provide 'Selected interpretations of *Cane*,' 'Women and Male-Female Relationships in *Cane*' and 'Celebration and Biblical Myth; Surrealism and Blues in *Cane*,' indicate most clearly the ways in which approaches to *Cane* had and would develop, focusing as they do on issues of race and gender, *Cane*'s relationship to other modernist movements and its fusion of popular and folk forms and themes.

Robert B. Jones' *Jean Toomer and the Prison-house of Thought: A Phenomenology of the Spirit* (1993) is a sustained attempt to relate the whole of Toomer's *oeuvre* to identifiable stages of spiritual and philosophical development. As Jones writes, he examined 'the vast network of published and unpublished texts' by Toomer, so that he 'was able to assign specific works to periods in Toomer's intellectual development.'[1] This development is plotted against Søren Kierkegaard's stages of spiritual evolution in which the writing of *Cane* corresponds to the first or 'aesthetic' stage of development, and this section includes some interesting insights into Toomer's modernist experimentation. Works produced from 1924–39 fall into the Gurdjieff period which corresponds to Kierkegaard's 'Ethical Sphere,' and Toomer's final Quaker writings fall into the 'Religious Sphere.'

---

1 Robert B. Jones, *Jean Toomer and the Prison-house of Thought: A Phenomenology of the Spirit* (Amherst: University of Massachusetts Press, 1993), p. xiii.

Jones' text deploys philosophical and theoretical concepts skilfully, arguing that Toomer's resistance to the reification of abstract categories such as race forced him into an opposed philosophical idealism and mysticism which, paradoxically, forced him to reify an idealised version of himself 'beyond' race. The treatment of Toomer's early artistic development, and of *Cane* itself, however, takes up less than a third of the study, as the emphasis falls on Toomer's later and critically neglected published and unpublished works and how they correspond to the trajectory of his philosophical and religious development.

A much more socially and historically grounded study is Charles Scruggs and Lee Vandemarr's *Jean Toomer and the Terrors of American History* (1998), which concentrates on *Cane* and the early work and the thinking that provided the foundation for it. As Scruggs and Vandemarr are at pains to show, these foundations are political and social:

> Although by the end of 1923 Toomer was on his way to embracing Gurdjieffism, this future choice is largely irrelevant to Cane's meaning. The 'spiritual' always appears in Cane within a political context, that is, within a context concerned with issues involving the American polis.[1]

In order to demonstrate its position *Jean Toomer and the Terrors of American History* reproduces Toomer's early political essays (as has been noted, essays which he himself fails to acknowledge in his own autobiographical writings), provides a wealth of contextual detail regarding the historical trends and racial discourses of the time, and analyses Toomer's early works in terms of their response to these factors. The 'terrors' of American history—the 'primal crime' of slavery, the horrors of racism, the illogical prevalence and shame of miscegenation—contribute to what the study argues is 'the Gothic horror story that Toomer told in *Cane*' (p. 111). Contexts and influences as well as issues of class, race and gender provide the historical and conceptual framework of the study. Toomer's relationship with the

---

1   Scruggs and Vandemarr, *Jean Toomer and the Terrors of American History*, p. 4.

Harlem Renaissance gets full coverage, but so does his position in the group that included Waldo Frank, Sherwood Anderson and other 'lost generation' American modernists. Toomer's own conflict over matters of racial identity and cultural belonging are treated in detail, and are mapped onto tensions and conflicts in the culture at large, and throughout, Scruggs and Vandemarr are at pains to provide textual evidence for their arguments and insights.

Because of its emphasis upon the ways in which *Cane* confronts the brutality of American history in its pages, the study's conclusions about Toomer's work stress the bleakness of its message. In *Jean Toomer, Artist* Nellie McKay had seen redemption in the 'Gold-glowing child' of the book's final lines. *Jean Toomer and the Terrors of American History* notes how in these lines 'images that have been associated with miscegenation and death—cradle, treetops, pines, child, birth—are now transformed into a 'birth-song' of hope.' However, the authors insist that such hope is problematic, as everything in *Cane* that leads up to its conclusion 'contradicts such optimism' (p. 203) and the desolate events in the Gothic cellar of 'Kabnis' ensure that *Cane*'s final lines offer only an ironic redemption. Taking the incomplete arcs or curves that preface each of *Cane*'s subdivisions as a structural and creative metaphor, Scruggs and Vandemarr argue that Toomer's attempts to 'complete' the curves of *Cane* fail. In the book's final moments Kabnis trudges upstairs:

> The poet's light has gone out, his center of gravity is lost. The two words that Father John gives him are 'sin' and 'death,' the legacy of slavery whose circle of eternal recurrence must be broken. This is something that Kabnis cannot do, and that Toomer can do only by forming a new circle that excludes Kabnis (p. 206).

That new circle would be sought in the Gurdjeffian teachings which would, for good or ill, rescue Toomer from *Cane*'s Gothic cellar.

Geneviève Fabre and Michael Feith's collection *Jean Toomer and the Harlem Renaissance* (2001) presents thirteen essays which focus on *Cane* and earlier works by Toomer.¹ Historical and literary contexts, racial discourse and racial identity, passing, Toomer and the musical, visual and dramatic arts, myth, dream and eugenics— these and other topics are covered in a volume whose approaches vary from a close textual analysis of a single sketch to a review of publisher Horace Liveright's advertising practices. Special mention might be given to George Hutchinson's essay 'Identity in Motion: Placing *Cane*' here, if only because Hutchinson's work is always illuminating and has been at the forefront of endeavours to draw out the nuances of Toomer's racial politics by closely examining the historical contexts and racial discourses of the time. (Please see the bibliography for some of Hutchinson's relevant publications).

Karen Jackson Ford's *Split-Gut Song: Jean Toomer and the Poetics of Modernity* (2005), is a model of close reading and manages to give an exhaustive examination of *Cane*—from both formal and thematic angles—by using the text's poetry as a way in to Toomer's modernist experimentation. Ford's introduction argues that readings of *Cane*'s poetry will go against the grain of critical opinion, in that 'the poetry of *Cane* tells quite a different story from the one many readers have sought in its pages, a story not of awakening, reconciliation, or promise but one of nostalgia, fragmentation, defeat.'² As this short overview of critical assessments of *Cane* might have suggested, Ford's verdicts of 'nostalgia, fragmentation, defeat' are actually in line with the majority of recent critical findings. What Ford's volume actually achieves is an intelligent journey through Toomer's text showing how the poetry and its forms—and the poetry is often more traditionally grounded than readers might realise—participates in *Cane*'s dialogic processes, modifying its meanings and intensifying its allusions in ways that only poetry can, and in ways that that Ford's study helps the reader to see. The complex interplay between genres that *Cane* performs is always at the focal point of Ford's discussions, and she shows that from the outset Toomer's work is generating complex

---

1 Geneviève Fabre and Michael Feith (eds) *Jean Toomer and the Harlem Renaissance* (New Jersey and London: Rutgers University Press, 2001).
2 Ford, *Split-Gut Song*, pp. 2–3.

levels of meaning from the interaction between prose and poetry—providing complex formalist readings that complement Scruggs and Vandemarr's historical accounts of the 'terrors' of American history:

> Prose is the discourse of realism, modernity, and tragedy; poetry of idealism, the past, and hope. As we've already seen in 'Karintha,' of course, the book does not always keep its generic modes apart. Eruptions of lyric in the prose sections suggest the book's pained intolerance of its own desire for realistic representation. Lyric functions at these times like whistling in the dark; its role is to repudiate the tragic facts of African American life in the modern world through a lyricism that is often more macabre than consoling (p. 43).

Ford announces at the outset that poetry and song are *Cane*'s privileged forms (p. 8) and this perception does alter the reading of the text in significant and relevant ways. Ford's first chapter situates Toomer's writing in the context of modernist poetics, and her closing chapter looks briefly at Toomer's later poems, and especially 'The Blue Meridian,' but her study gives a chapter to each of *Cane*'s subdivisions, performing interpretations which are exemplary in their attention to the details of the language and forms of Toomer's greatest work.

6. Bibliography

6.1 Works by Jean Toomer

Toomer, Jean, *Cane*, edited by Darwin W. Turner (New York & London: W. W. Norton, 1988).

—— *Cane*, second edition, edited by Rudolph P. Byrd and Henry Louis Gates Jr. (New York & London: W. W. Norton, 2011). The Norton editions include extensive contextual and biographical essays, contemporary reviews, extracts from relevant autobiographical writings and correspondence, and generous selections of contemporaneous and recent critical essays. These editions are highly recommended.

—— 'Balo', in James V. Hatch and Ted Shine (eds), *Black Theatre USA: Plays by African Americans 1847 to Today* (New York and London: The Free Press, 1996), pp. 223–30.

—— *A Jean Toomer Reader: Selected Unpublished Writings*, edited by Frederik L. Rusch (New York & Oxford: Oxford University Press, 1993). This volume presents a range of published and unpublished writings—letters, poems, stories, a play, autobiographical pieces and essays—arranged thematically. Sections include writings relating to *Cane*, racial identity and the 'new' race, writings inspired by the teachings of Georges Gurdjieff, and writings on America and its landscapes.

—— *Brother Mine: The Correspondence of Jean Toomer and Waldo Frank*, edited by Kathleen Pfeiffer (Urbana: University of Illinois Press, 2010).

—— *Selected Essays and Literary Criticism*, edited by Robert B. Jones (Knoxville: The University of Tennessee Press, 1996). A useful collection of Toomer's essays, arranged into sections on literary criticism and reviews, cultural and sociological criticism, and essays on his turn to Quakerism.

—— *The Letters of Jean Toomer 1919–1924*, edited by Mark Whalan (Knoxville: University of Tennessee Press, 2006)

—— *The Wayward and the Seeking: A Collection of Writings by Jean Toomer*, edited by Darwin W. Turner (Washington D. C.: Howard University Press, 1982). Although some of this material has now been made available elsewhere, this volume is still the most comprehensive collection of Toomer's autobiographical sketches, fiction, poetry and drama.

6.2 Secondary Works

Anderson, Sherwood, *Winesburg, Ohio* (Oxford: Oxford University Press, 1997).

Benson, Brian Joseph, and Mabel Mayle Dillard, *Jean Toomer* (Boston: Twayne Publishers, 1980). The first full-length study of Toomer's work. The study cites a lot of material that was then generally unavailable in order to detail Toomer's growth as an artist and his struggle with ideas of race and racial identity. A lot of space is given over to Toomer's post-*Cane* spiritual quest and writings, but at the centre of the study is a detailed discussion of *Cane* which takes a section-by-section approach to the work and draws attention to textual features such as its lyrical prose style complex shifts in points of view.

Bone, Robert A., *The Negro Novel in America* (New Haven: Yale University Press, 1958).

Bowen, Barbara E., 'Untroubled Voice: Call and Response in *Cane,'* in Henry Louis Gates Jr (ed.), *Black Literature and Literary Theory* (London: Methuen, 1984), pp. 187–203. Bowen uses the call and response vocal structure found in the blues, gospel music, and African American religious ceremonies, to show that a key aspect of *Cane* is the "gesture of listening for a voice", or a response to a call. *Cane*'s valorisation of folk song is well known, but Bowen maps the call and response scheme onto the work's sketches and poems in convincing and illuminating ways, showing that *Cane* is suffused by voices and calls which wait in vain for a response.

Chapman, Abraham (ed.), *Black Voices: An Anthology of Afro-American Literature* (New York: New American Library, 1968).

du Bois, W .E. B, *The Souls of Black Folk* (Harmondsworth: Penguin, 1996).

—— *Du Bois On Education*, edited by Eugene F. Provenzo (Walnut Creek C. A.: AltaMira Press, 2002).

Durham, Frank (ed.), *The Merrill Studies in 'Cane'* (Columbus: Charles E. Merrill Publishing, 1971). The first collection of essays on Toomer, bringing together early reviews, essays and introductions as well as new critical essays and extracts from relevant studies of black American writing.

Fabre, Geneviève and Michael Feith (eds) *Jean Toomer and the Harlem Renaissance* (New Jersey and London: Rutgers University Press, 2001). The most recent collection of 13 essays on Toomer, all of which focus on *Cane* and the works and contextual issues that produced it and ensured its position in the Harlem Renaissance.

Fahy, Thomas, 'The Enslaving Power of Folksong in Jean Toomer's *Cane*,' in Michael J. Meyer (ed.) *Literature and Music, Rodopi Perspectives on Modern Literature 25* (Amsterdam and New York: Rodopi, 2002), pp. 47–63.

Ford, Karen Jackson, *Split-Gut Song: Jean Toomer and the Poetics of Modernity* (Tuscaloosa: The University of Alabama Press, 2005). Although the focus of Ford's study is the poetry and poetics of Toomer's work, her insights into the themes and forms of the verse allow her to conduct incisive and insightful close readings of *Cane*'s prose and drama, as well as a range of his other works, that cast fresh light on *Cane*'s ingenuity and complexity. Ford dedicates a chapter to the 'Poet and Poetry After *Cane*', but the centre of the study is Toomer's problematic poetic 'novel', its experiments with language, and its concern with the fate of the lyric and the record of African-American experience that lyric enshrined, in the modern world.

Frank, Waldo, *Our America* (New York: Boni and Liveright, 1919).

Frost, Robert. *North of Boston* (Charleston: Nabu Press, 2011).

Griffin, Farah Jasmine, *Who Set You Flowin'? The African-American Migration Narrative* (New York and Oxford: Oxford University Press, 1995).

Hamilton, Marybeth, *In Search of the Blues* (New York: Basic Books, 2008).

Hutchinson, George, *The Harlem Renaissance in Black and White* (Cambridge Mass.: Harvard University Press, 1995).

—— 'Identity in Motion: Placing *Cane*,' in Fabre and Fleiss (eds), *Jean Toomer and the Harlem Renaissance*, pp. 38–56. In this and other essays Hutchinson fuses informed readings of the Toomer's work with authoritative analyses of the nuanced political, social and racial milieu in which the writings were produced. Here, Hutchinson looks at Toomer's biography, his relationship with writers like Waldo Frank and Sherwood Anderson, and the influence of Gurdjieff—while paying special attention to the fate of the 'mulatto' in early twentieth-century American legislation — in order to throw light upon the ways in which Toomer had to negotiate a complex racial identity for himself, and produce in *Cane* a work that needs to be read against the background of both white and black literary movements and traditions.

—— 'Jean Toomer and the 'New Negroes' of Washington,' *American Literature* 63: 41 (December 1991); reprinted in Byrd and Gates Jr (eds), *Cane*, second edition, pp. 305–12.

—— 'Jean Toomer and American Racial Discourse,' *Texas Studies in Literature and Language*, 35: 2 (Summer 1993), pp. 226–50.

—— (ed.) *The Cambridge Companion to the Harlem Renaissance* (Cambridge and New York: Cambridge University Press, 2007).

Jackson, Kevin, *Constellation of Genius 1922: Modernism Year One* (London: Hutchinson, 2012).

Johnson, Georgia Douglas Camp, *Bronze: A Book of Verse* (Boston: B. J. Brimmer Company, 1922).

Jones, Robert, B., *Jean Toomer and the Prison-house of Thought: A Phenomenology of the Spirit* (Amherst: University of Massachusetts Press, 1993). A heavily theorised approach to Toomer's *oeuvre* which is useful despite the relatively small space allotted to the discussion of *Cane* and Toomer's artistic development up until its publication. Despite this, the study deserves credit for its focus on Toomer's later, critically neglected published and unpublished works, and their relationship to the development of his later thought and beliefs.

Kerman, Cynthia Earl, and Richard Eldridge, *The Lives of Jean Toomer: A Hunger for Wholeness* (Baton Rouge and London: Louisiana State University Press, 1987). So far, this is the only full biography of Toomer. It is extremely useful on issues of race and Toomer's hankering for spiritual answers for his conflicted sense of identity, but its focus lies on Toomer's 'divided self,' and devotes relatively little space to *Cane* and its influences.

Larson, Charles R., *Invisible Darkness: Jean Toomer and Nella Larsen* (Iowa: University of Iowa Press, 1993). An interesting comparative treatment of two of the period's most enigmatic 'mixed race' authors, but it tends to be overly biographical in its approach and its treatment of Toomer's fiction suffers because of the study's rather erratic non-chronological structure.

Lempriere, J., *Lempriere's Classical Dictionary* (London: Bracken Books, 1984).

Lewis, David Levering (ed.), *The Portable Harlem Renaissance Reader* (Viking Penguin: New York and London, 1995).

Locke, Alain (ed.), *The New Negro* (New York: Touchstone Books, 1997).

McKay, Nellie Y., *Jean Toomer, Artist: A Study of His Literary Life and Work, 1894–1936* (Chapel Hill and London: The University of North Carolina Press, 1984). This is still one of the most useful studies of Toomer's work. Merging biographical discussion with his development as an artist, McKay looks at Toomer's early work as investigations of racial politics and African-American folk culture which would provide the vital impulses for the prose and poetry of *Cane*. The readings of *Cane* are especially thorough, and McKay blends issues raised by Toomer's own sense of racial crisis with readings of *Cane*'s themes and textual strategies in ways that still offer the most fruitful approaches to his text. The Gurdjieff years and Toomer's later 'polemical' writings are discussed, but the focus and value of McKay's study lies in its analysis of *Cane* and the influences which helped to produce it.

O'Daniel, Therman, B. (ed.), *Jean Toomer: A Critical Evaluation* (Washington: Howard University Press, 1988). Although out of print, this large volume comprises 46 valuable biographical and contextual essays and critical analyses, organised into sections which cover the whole of Toomer's life and writing career. The majority of the sections deal with *Cane*, its context and origins.

Pound, Ezra, *The Literary Essays of Ezra Pound*, edited by T. S. Eliot (London: Faber and Faber, 1985).

Scruggs, Charles and Lee Vandemarr, *Jean Toomer and the Terrors of American History* (Philadelphia: University of Pennsylvania Press, 1998). The focus of this study is on Toomer's reaction to the social and political conditions of his time and the ways in which these influenced his writing—with a special emphasis on the composition of *Cane* and the works that preceded it. Scruggs and Vandemarr go to great lengths to correct some of Toomer's deeply unreliable autobiographical writings and 'refashionings' of his life, and stress the ways in which his writing confronts the violence — racism, slavery, lynching, rape and miscegenation—of his epoch. Despite their dark characterisation of *Cane* as a 'gothic horror story' their analysis throws new light on Toomer's life, work, politics, and a range of concerns which his own later 'spiritual' accounts of his life tended to elide. An extensively researched and authoritative study.

Seldon, Raman, Peter Widdowson and Peter Brooker, *A Reader's Guide to Contemporary Literary Theory*, 5th edition (Hemel Hempstead: Harvester Wheatsheaf, 2005).

Sollers, Werner, 'Jean Toomer's *Cane*: Modernism and Race in Interwar America,' in Geneviève Fabre and Michael Feith (eds) *Jean Toomer and the Harlem Renaissance*, pp. 18–37.

Thurman, Wallace (ed.), *Fire!! Devoted to Younger Negro Artists*, 1: 1 (1926); reprinted by New Jersey: The Fire!! Press, 1982.

Waldron, Edward E., 'The Search for Identity in Jean Toomer's 'Esther,'' in Therman, B. O'Daniel (ed.), *Jean Toomer: A Critical Evaluation*, pp. 273–6.

Walker, Alice, *In Search of Our Mothers' Gardens* (London: The Women's Press, 1984). Walker's short essay, 'The Divided Life of Jean Toomer,' is significant in that for many people it was their first introduction to *Cane*, and while praising the work's beauty she chides the author for his irresponsibility in attempting to 'fling off racial labels.' Here Walker provided a 'divided' assessment of Toomer which still dominates discussion of his life and work.

Whalan, Mark, 'Jean Toomer and the avant-garde,' in George Hutchinson (ed.), *The Cambridge Companion to the Harlem Renaissance*, pp. 71–81.

Williams, William Carlos, *The Autobiography of William Carlos Williams* (New York: New Directions, 1967).

The Author

Dr Gerry Carlin is a Senior Lecturer in English at the University of Wolverhampton. He teaches, researches and has published in the areas of modernism, critical theory, and the literature and culture of the 1960s.

Humanities-Ebooks.co.uk

All Humanities Ebooks titles are available to Libraries through EBSCO and MyiLibrary.com

Some Academic titles

Sibylle Baumbach, *Shakespeare and the Art of Physiognomy*
John Beer, *Blake's Humanism*
John Beer, *The Achievement of E M Forster*
John Beer, *Coleridge the Visionary*
Jared Curtis, ed., *The Fenwick Notes of William Wordsworth**
Jared Curtis, ed., *The Cornell Wordsworth: A Supplement**
Steven Duncan, *Analytic Philosophy of Religion: its History since 1955**
John K Hale, *Milton as Multilingual: Selected Essays 1982–2004*
Simon Hull, ed., *The British Periodical Text, 1797–1835*
Rob Johnson, Mark Levene and Penny Roberts, eds., *History at the End of the World **
John Lennard, *Modern Dragons and other Essays on Genre Fiction**
C W R D Moseley, *Shakespeare's History Plays*
Paul McDonald, *Laughing at the Darkness: Postmodernism and American Humour **
Colin Nicholson, *Fivefathers: Interviews with late Twentieth-Century Scottish Poets*
W J B Owen, *Understanding 'The Prelude'*
Pamela Perkins, ed., *Francis Jeffrey's Highland and Continental Tours**
Keith Sagar, *D. H. Lawrence: Poet**
Reinaldo Francisco Silva, *Portuguese American Literature**
William Wordsworth, *Concerning the Convention of Cintra**
W J B Owen and J W Smyser, eds., *Wordsworth's Political Writings**
The Poems of William Wordsworth: Collected Reading Texts from the Cornell Wordsworth, 3 vols.*

* These titles are also available in print using links from
http://www.humanities-ebooks.co.uk

Humanities Insights

These are some of the Insights available at:
http://www.humanities-ebooks.co.uk/

General Titles

An Introduction to Critical Theory
Modern Feminist Theory
An Introduction to Rhetorical Terms

Genre FictionSightlines

Octavia E Butler: *Xenogenesis / Lilith's Brood*
Reginal Hill: *On Beulah's Height*
Ian McDonald: *Chaga / Evolution's Store*
Walter Mosley: *Devil in a Blue Dress*
Tamora Pierce: *The Immortals*
Tamora Pierce: *Protector of the Small*

History Insights

Oliver Cromwell
The British Empire: Pomp, Power and Postcolonialism
The Holocaust: Events, Motives, Legacy
Lenin's Revolution
Methodism and Society
The Risorgimento

Literature Insights

Austen: *Emma*
Conrad: *The Secret Agent*
T S Eliot: 'The Love Song of J Alfred Prufrock' and *The Waste Land*
English Renaissance Drama: Theatre and Theatres in Shakespeare's Time
Faulkner: *Go Down, Moses* and *Big Woods'*
Faulkner: *The Sound and the Fury*
Gaskell, *Mary Barton*
Hardy: *Tess of the Durbervilles*
Heller: *Catch-22*
Ibsen: *The Doll's House*
Hopkins: Selected Poems
Hughes: *New Selected Poems*
Larkin: *Selected Poems*
Lawrence: Selected Short Stories
Lawrence: *Sons and Lovers*
Lawrence: *Women in Love*
Morrison: *Beloved*

Scott: *The Raj Quartet*
Shakespeare: *Hamlet*
Shakespeare: *Henry IV*
Shakespeare: *King Lear*
Shakespeare: *Richard II*
Shakespeare: *Richard III*
Shakespeare: *The Merchant of Venice*
Shakespeare: *The Tempest*
Shakespeare: *Troilus and Cressida*
Shelley: *Frankenstein*
Wordsworth: *Lyrical Ballads*
Fields of Agony: English Poetry and the First World War

Philosophy Insights

Agamben
American Pragmatism
Barthes
Thinking Ethically about Business
Critical Thinking
Existentialism
Formal Logic
Metaethics
Contemporary Philosophy of Religion
Philosophy of Sport
Plato
Wittgenstein
Žižek

Some Titles in Preparation

Philosophy of Mind
Political Psychology
Rousseau's legacy

Austen: *Pride and Prejudice*
Blake: *Songs of Innocence & Experience*
Chatwin: *In Patagonia*
Dreiser: *Sister Carrie*
Eliot, George: *Silas Marner*
Eliot: *Four Quartets*
Fitzgerald: *The Great Gatsby*
Hardy: Selected Poems
Heaney: Selected Poems
James: *The Ambassadors*
Lawrence: *The Rainbow*
Melville: *Moby-Dick*
Melville: Three Novellas
Shakespeare: *Macbeth*
Shakespeare: *Romeo and Juliet*
Shakespeare: *Twelfth Night*